A WALK INTO THE VOID

A Walk into the Void

WRITTEN BY ABDUL AKBARYEH

Art by Edy Rios

AHAauthor

Dedicated to my loving
wife Emily that helped
keep me motivated and
wouldn't let me give
up before even trying.

Also in dedication of my
family and friends that
have always read my
drafts throughout the
years!

CONTENTS

$$\sim \text{I} \sim$$

AGAINST THE BLIZZARD

I was speeding down the road against a blizzard. Mother Nature showed me her teeth as I haughtily kept increasing my speed. First 25, then 45, and before I knew it, I had hit 80 miles per hour. The small vehicle shook as I fought to keep control. Toyota Corollas were not made for these conditions. I kept nervously looking over my shoulder and in the rear-view mirror. No one had been following me for the last couple hours; no one is crazy enough to follow me into this storm. I steadied my breath, counted to ten, and calmed myself down. I began to apply the brakes until I brought the speed of my car back down to 30 miles per hour. As the car slowed down, so did my heart rate, and breathing.

My windshield wipers swished back and forth with panic as the snow came faster and faster. The car rattled as I drove against Mother Nature's rage. She was angry, but there was nothing I could do to appease her. I looked into the mirror to see my troubled hazel eyes and long curly brown hair, now in disarray. If it were not for the creases around my mouth and eyes, I would be considered youthful.

The initial adrenaline rush finally came to end and I grew tired of the highway so I took an exit, more rural scenery would help put my mind at ease, I thought. I took another deep breath as I looked out to my left through a cloudy window for a glimpse of Jack Frost's wonderland. White covered the trees, and with every breeze a huge chunk of snow would fall off nearby branches and onto the ground with an audible thud. I scanned the road before me and could not see much more than a deer's hoof prints on the road; I was completely alone surrounded by a surreal frozen forest.

The only sounds were the hum of the engine, the grind of tires against a rugged road covered in dense snow, and the gentle tap of falling snow. I began to feel lonely in the silence and my mind began to drift to her and the first time we met.

I can still imagine her leaning against our tree, the place where we met as teenagers. The tree towered higher than any house I had seen and had a thick trunk that a child could easily hide behind. The bark was thick and brown, and it was filled with strong branches filled with bright green leaves. The tree felt full of life and warmth.

I was taking a stroll around the neighborhood after taking out the trash. Feeling a bit adventurous, I ventured into the woods near our house. I was crunching orange and red leaves, gaining a small satisfaction from my noisy steps until I heard a faint whimper. I turned and looked toward the tree and I saw her huddled under a large oak tree.

It's amazing how life turns out. Annabel and I grew up in the same town, but we never met until a chilly day in autumn under our tree. She was running away from home; it was another night where her drunken mother would blurt out nonsense to anyone in the vicinity and she couldn't take the unwarranted punishment anymore. She sat under the tree with her beautiful face buried in her knees, weeping, and wondering why fate was so cruel to her.

The bark was strained with centuries of age. If only that tree could speak, it would have an unbelievable story to tell. Hearts were carved into the bark, some low, some high, and one was just above Annabel's head. Her hair looked silky and soft. I automatically felt drawn to her. I swept down and picked up a dandelion as I walked over to her.

The car jumped up and slammed back down from a speed bump hidden under the snow. The thud woke me up from the daze. The snow kept falling harder and harder with every passing minute, but I was still far from where I needed to be. I prayed to God for somewhere safe to stay for the night, but all I saw were woods and a twisted road ahead of me. It was beautiful to behold the boulders jutting out of the hillside beside me and the iced lake, but my concern grew as my vehicle began to slide even at 20 miles per hour. The snow just wouldn't relent. Before me was a two-way road with one lane coming and one lane going. Thankfully, there was no traffic as I slid between the two lanes, struggling to avoid the ledge.

I needed my full concentration to navigate the road, but my mind was no longer in a stable place. Tears began to fog my vision. I would swipe my gloves at my eyes to dry them, but the dam was broken. The memories flooded into my mind, her smile, her eyes daring me forward, her warmth, her kindness, her tears, my tears. I strained my eyes to see reality in front of me, but the memories of the past were mixing with the chaos of the blizzard. I struggled to see the road, now covered entirely with snow with no lane markers in site.

The car buckled and heaved; the steering wheel whipped itself out of my trembling hands. I was sobbing uncontrollably as the car was going down a steep, icy hill. The car began to spin down the hill but was still on the road. After the first rotation, a feeling of sheer panic overtook me. My muscles tightened and my hair stood on end, as I realized what a mess I was in. With tears still running out of my eyes, I took a firm hold of the steering wheel and began to slowly pump the brakes. I made sure to avoid sudden motions as I pulled the wheel against the turns. The brakes squeaked like a mouse chased by a cat.

The car was beginning to calm down again, but my head was spinning from the shock. My hand jerked to the right subconsciously and my car's wheels slid off the road. I looked out of my windshield and saw the rolling hill under me, covered in snow with scattered trees and rocks. My heart jumped into my mouth. The car tipped over nose first so I could witness the horror before me. The tires made a scraping noise, struggling for a moment against the snow of the road, trying to hold on, but the momentum of the car was already set toward my doom. The whole car swung violently forward and bounced as the tires collided with the ground.

I was done trying to fight this. There was nothing left to fight for behind me and too much to fight against ahead of me. I closed my eyes and prayed for mercy. The car managed to roll down the hill against my will and propelled me toward an impending violent collision. The car shook like a raft against a raging river. There was nothing left but to hope I would be given the privilege of a swift and painless death.

With my eyes closed, my mind drifted back again to my constant. I was only a few steps from her as she sat at the foot of that great oak tree. I sat down beside her and put my arm around her delicate shoulder. She withdrew from my arm and scooted away. She raised her head from her knees and glared at me with wild eyes, running with tears. I brought a dandelion forward toward this nymph as a tribute to her beauty. Her expression softened and the sobbing relented as she took the flower with a faint smile on her face. From that moment on I wanted nothing other than to make her smile.

"Hey, you're that girl from chemistry class, right? What are you doing out here crying all alone? I always felt crying is better when there's someone to talk to or else it'll just be a sad wheel that keeps turning until you really get those feelings out in words..." It was stupid, but it was all I could come up with at the time. I wasn't expecting to find a cute girl on a random walk. When I looked into her eyes, I saw in their depths an essence full of warmth; it wanted to see the world, to love unconditionally, to give kindness, but right now those eyes were filled with great pain.

Her faint smile grew, and her chest rose as she gave a soft chuckle. She wiped off her tears with her sleeve. I can still remember her royal blue sweater as if it were a recent memory. "Well, a couple months ago... My... My father died... He was a police officer and he... He just wanted to help him..."

She was starting to look as gloomy as before I came. "I bet he was a great man," I added as she struggled with her words. She shook her head in agreement with a gentle smile.

"Yes, he was, but now my mom has lost it! She's just so condescending, we all lost our father, and we need her to be there for us. Instead, she's drinking herself into a frenzy of cursing and angry rants. I can't take it anymore! I just want it to end!" Her little body began to shudder again and her eyes started to glisten.

"This seems rough now, but take it from me, life gets better." Just some stupid adage I heard somewhere from optimists. At the time, I scarcely knew a thing about hardship. They were shallow words, but I would have said anything to get her to find hope again.

"And if it doesn't?" she challenged.

"It will, I know it will," I replied with confidence. I could feel that she was something special; she stirred up feelings in me that I had never felt before. I felt an inexplicable warmth in my chest, an incredible compassion for this fallen angel.

"How are you so sure? How can you be such an optimist?"

I struggled with the question and dug deep for a genuine answer instead of some meaningless thing I read in a hundred books. What did I believe in that kept me going? "No one ever said life was going to be easy. But when it gets hard, you can't just give up. When things get a little rough, we can't forget how sweet the highs can be. As Aristotle once said, it is during our darkest moments that we must focus to see the light. The light never dies." It still wasn't a full answer, but I was younger then.

"It gets hard sometimes... I miss him so much... I can't stand the way things are," deep in her beautiful eyes, I began to see dejection again.

"He's not gone. As long as you carry his memory inside of you, he's not gone completely. I lost my grandmother a year ago. It was a hard time for everyone, especially my dad. We got through it though, together. Together we kept her memory alive by remembering her words of wisdom and by remembering the many happy times we had spent with her. We are all bound to each other, like a tree and its roots," I said as I looked at the magnificent tree she leaned upon. Then my gaze fell to her eyes and her eyes gazed back into mine. Her look melted my heart; I was lost in the aura of her green eyes, bright green like granny smith apples. She wrapped her small fingers around my hand and held tight, lowering her head onto my shoulder. "Don't give up, never give up," I whispered into her ear as we watched the sunset together. Her problems didn't really go away for a while, but at least she found some relief for the moment. Some therapy and college really made the biggest difference for her.

Metal pushed through snapping branches and scraped against a tree trunk with a horrible screech that shook me away from the distant shores of sweet memories. Death was not far now, soon now the next impact wouldn't be a scrape but the collision that would end me. My eyes were closed tight as my head rocked and collided with my seat and with the window beside me. It felt like my head would burst as a world of darkness spun around me. Through the loud crashes and bangs, I heard her gentle voice whisper in my ear just loud enough to be heard. *"Don't give up, never give up."* My breath stopped for a moment from the sound of her voice. It was like she was just beside me.

Deep inside, I could feel my heartbeat with more warmth than it had in a while. The beating of the drum of life started again. I opened my eyes wide against all reason. I saw a large pile of snow fall from a tree branch above onto my windshield, it sounded more like the swing of a metal bat than snow. The car continued barreling down the hill. I took a deep breath and looked to my right and my left. To my right I noticed a small town across a wooden bridge. I couldn't make out much due to the heavy snowfall impeding my vision, but from what I could tell, the houses seemed grey and tattered. There were a few cars parked in front of houses, mostly trucks, but I did not see anyone out on the streets. They seemed wiser than me.

I drew my head forward, ignoring the pain in my neck and back from the turbulent ride. The windshield wipers threw off the latest batch of snow, revealing a ledge with a drop off a mere fifty yards ahead of me. I frantically unclipped my seat belt, opened the door, and then threw myself out the door as the car began to accumulate momentum. I rolled onto the soft snow and I grabbed at the ground in an attempt to stop myself from following my car off the ledge. A rock cut the top of my right brow and I raised my arms to defend my face from a fallen branch a moment before I rolled through it. Its sharp ends tried to dig themselves into my arms, but to no avail against my thick winter coat. I reached and grabbed handfuls of snow, slowing down my brutal descent. The car fell off the ledge with a horrible creak which resulted in an alarming crash that shook the earth. I could hear owls waking from their slumber and flying away in a state of shock. The whole woods erupted with the sounds of animals flying and running away from the unnatural ruckus. I was lucky enough to stop falling down the hill as my hands grabbed firmly to the ground through the thick layer of snow.

I was panting and laughing once I realized I was still alive. The temperature was dropping and so was the sun. I wanted to lay there in the snow, but I knew I would freeze in the harsh night. I gingerly stood up and dusted off my brown suede jacket and jeans with my leather gloves. Part of me still couldn't believe I was alive. The sting of the artic wind against my eyes and cheeks was convincing evidence. My body was still shaking with adrenaline but as the sun continued to set, I knew there was no time left to stand idly by. I looked out to my right to the small town, my next destination. It seemed like a cute middle of nowhere kind of town with no building over two stories and a healthy supply of small shops and mostly single-family houses. There was a gas station at the edge of town. I saw a rough path I could take to reach the bridge that crossed the river and led to the town.

I lifted my hiking boots out of the deep snow gingerly and began to trudge toward the village. I was still shaking from the crash through the trees, or perhaps I was just cold, it was hard to tell. My nose felt numb, but the rest of my body felt warm under my coat, even against the ravaging wind. Speckles of white dust were blown into my eyes, and I squinted against nature's onslaught.

The path was even enough to travel upon without much difficulty except a few scattered tree stumps and buried stones. An exceptionally large rock caught my foot and I stumbled forward. I saved myself from falling face first into the snow by grabbing onto a nearby low hanging branch. As I pulled on the branch, a heap of snow fell onto my head. It felt like a bucket of ice as the snow slid onto my neck from my head. I chuckled, remembering playful winters with Annabel, throwing snowballs at each other. I shook the snow out of my light brown hair and continued on my way. I took a deep breath in and exhaled a white cloud as I drifted back into memories to protect me from the reality around me.

We were in the house after an energetic bout in the snow. She wrapped me in a hand knit blanket, knit by her grandmother. It had leaf patterns all around a central tree; it reminded me of fall with its shades of brown and dark red. Annabel came through the kitchen door with two dark blue mugs with swirls of steam dancing over the top of them. She nudged me to the side with her hip as she settled down onto the sofa next to me. She smiled at me, kissed me on the forehead and handed me the mug of hot cocoa with whipped crème and chocolate syrup in the shape of a heart. I kissed her back on the cheek and cheerfully took a small sip of the hot drink. It warmed my whole body and took the numbness out of my cheeks. I wrapped my arms around her little shoulders as she turned on the television and rested her head onto my chest.

"I knew we would be happy here honey," she said in her gentle voice. It was Annabel's idea to buy a house together. It was a huge risk, we were both young and just starting to pay our college debts, but she believed that things would just "work out." After a year of discussing, she eventually won me over. In retrospect, I wish I would have listened to her sooner.

"Annabel, I'm happy wherever and whenever I am with you," I replied with a gentle kiss to the top of her golden head. I could smell her sweet lilac perfume, the sweetest smell in the world.

Today, as the light slowly faded, I could smell nothing but a faint scent of smoke. It smelled like the smoke of a fresh chunk of timber. Hopefully, the smoke came from the chimney of a house in the village, caused by a nice large fire, cooking a fresh steak. I began to salivate and the reality of my extreme weakness and hunger began to kick in. The trauma from the crash made me forget that my only meal for the day was breakfast, and even that had not been substantial.

I used branches to keep myself upright as I carefully made my way forward. Above me were tall, archaic trees. The woods were a panorama of nature's beauty in winter, but I failed to perceive any of its beauty. I was lost in fear, and in sweet memories of my love. Lost in darkness, I was chasing my source of light.

Ahead of me, I spotted a dark object behind a tree on the trail. I could not make sense of it. It looked like someone had hung a fine black coat made of lace on a tree. The coat seemed rather queer. I could feel a bitter breeze, but the coat did not sway with the wind. Inexplicably, this peculiar coat awoke an incredible sense of fear within me. It was an uncontrollable danger sense. The coat, if that was certainly all it was, did not belong out here in such horrible weather. The visibility was still awful, although the snow fall was starting to slow, the incumbent darkness made matters worse. I began to stumble more than before, but that eerie coat was still on my mind even as I turned my focus back to the trail.

The bridge was thankfully growing closer. The feeling of fear and anxiety kept clawing at the back of mind. I considered running to the village but with my overwhelming feeling of weakness and hunger in the cold, it would be too dangerous. It felt like any extra strain would exhaust my limits and I would simply collapse. I reassured myself that if I got through this, someone in town would indeed make me a steak or a beef stew and if not, there must be a restaurant somewhere in that town that's still open.

I nervously scanned the area, checking for any wild animals. Around me was an empty forest covered in white powder and the gentle tap of falling snow. Perhaps the coat was all that was left of a victim of a grizzly animal mauling. Visions of grizzly bears and bobcats danced in my head. Their muzzles dripping with blood from a fresh kill.

I closed my eyes tight and felt my body almost keel over from exhaustion. Visions overtook me like hallucinations in the cold. It was like something between a dream and memory. I was back in a lush forest with brown and red leaves falling around me with her by my side. "We'll make it through this place just fine," she said in her angelic voice. Her voice was still strong in my ears against the chilling autumn wind. I was always bad with directions, and once again I had managed to get us lost. We had spent the last four hours in the forest. It was supposed to be a one-hour hike.

Annabel had a fiery spirit; it was one of the things I loved most about her. Even though she knew we were lost, she was having a blast. We were adventurers exploring a new land that was full of mystery and awe. Her comfort eased my nerves, how could I feel like I'm in danger with her smiling so innocently?

I adored the beautiful shades of autumn upon the trees in the town of Pinetop-Lakeside. The leaves were a vibrant orange, almost glowing in the sun's rays. I heard a rustling behind us and I spun around to identify the oncoming threat. The bushes were now at my ten o'clock. My right hand swiftly reached for the Swiss army knife in my coat pocket. It wasn't much, an old memento from my father, but it was all I had on me.

I clutched the Swiss army knife as Annabel slowly turned, rolling her eyes with an amused look on her face. A black squirrel without a tail jumped out. It sniffed the air and looked right and left hurriedly. Its beady black eyes were clearly searching for something. Judging by the way it looked past us, it was neither me nor Annabel that it was looking for. Its black coal eyes settled on a point behind Annabel for an instant. The squirrel vanished immediately, hurriedly scurrying up the nearest tree with dark, thick bark.

I turned with my head cocked to the side, peering in the direction that awoke such fear in this friendly woodland critter, perhaps it's the same thing that took its tail. I saw nothing; there were some fern bushes and a few rows of large trees with protruding roots. Annabel began to hum a soft tune. She did not notice the squirrel's agitation the way I had. It was afraid of something, and that something was coming.

I listened closely for any sound. I brought a finger to my lips to quite Annabel and turned my right ear toward the bushes. I began to hear the crunch of autumn leaves in the distance. The crunching was getting continually louder, and it sounded like many heavy paws. I hoped it would be nothing more than a deer, but I could tell by the clunky steps that it was not a deer. I felt a light sweat on my brow as the crunching became louder and I began to hear panting.

My family told me stories about wolves; they always suggested standing your ground and showing confidence. I guess at the end of the day there was not much more anyone could do. Out running a pack of wolves was unlikely.

Anticipating wolves, I instinctually stepped in front of Annabel with my red Swiss army knife in my hand. She was the love of my life, and my girlfriend of four years at the time. I widened my eyes to see as much as possible. Wherever the sound was coming from, I would make sure to confront it for her. A group of four bloodhounds burst through the bushes in between the trees with their mouths wide open, dripping with thick, white slobber. At first glance, they looked more disgusting than threatening.

Looking in their eyes, I saw that these dogs were out here to hunt. I had no idea what they were looking for, but I knew one thing, I would not let these mutts hurt my love. I stood my ground, unflinching. In the corner of my eye, I saw a wisp of golden hair and the edge of a sharp nose. Annabel was standing beside me. "You're not alone," Annabel said in a firm voice. That was the moment I knew I wanted to marry her. She was more than the object of my affection; she was my partner.

The bloodhound on my far left had a particularly threatening look in its jet-black eyes. It snarled at us and showed its white canines in a show of force. The other three dogs seemed docile by comparison. They were all busy sniffing the air and the ground in every direction. Annabel and I drew closer to each other; we stood shoulder by shoulder. For me, feeling her shoulder against mine, although her shoulder trembled with fear, made me feel stronger. Many things terrify me, I am not brave or fearless by nature, but with her by my side, I was willing to face any beast and any trial.

In retrospect, my paranoia at that time was laughable. I was terrified of finding an animal in the woods, but there were apparently worse things afoot. The bloodhounds belonged to a sturdy police officer. The officer was a good foot taller than me, and a kind man. He smiled at us and apologized for startling us as he calmly emerged from the bushes, following his hounds. He explained to us that there were reports of a hunter venturing the woods, hunting a wild bear. Apparently, this hunter had not been heard of or seen for a full week, and his brother was also missing.

Recalling the memory helped calm me down. I reassured myself that there was nothing in the woods with me now worth fearing. One way or another, I knew I could make it to the village. I eased myself off the branch and continued to stagger down the snow-covered hill. The bridge was only a little way off from the foot of the hill. This long day may finally end, I thought to myself. The smell of burning timber became more and more inviting with every step forward.

As I continued, gingerly moving forward, I heard no twigs break save for those I broke. The loudest sounds now were the crunch of my boots into the hard snow. I saw no movement except for the branches I would push out of my way as I made my progress through the thick woods. Loneliness grasped my heart with its unpitying hands. It squeezed the warmth out of my body until I recalled the tangible memories of my love. It almost felt as if her warm hands were keeping my cheeks warm against the wind. As I remembered her warm embrace, strength returned to my body, and I kept moving.

I began hearing whispers, it felt like they were coming from the trees all around me. At first, I ignored them, dismissed the whispers as the wind. As I carefully staggered forward, the whispers became hoarse and I could make out some of the morbid words. "Death begets death... run.... hide ..... No good... You will be found.... All in time... Time.... Time...Time...."

I froze in place, my body was numb with unprecedented fear so deep that I could taste a strange bitterness on my tongue and feel a chill throughout my entire body, permeating to my bones. Suddenly, it felt as though I may never make it to the village. My arm began to tremble uncontrollably from the feeling of dread. The last words still echoed, resonating like a sinister melody.

I willed myself to look around for a source to the hoarse whispers. There was nothing around me save a black coat behind a tree off to my right. The coat gave me the same eerie feeling as before and seemed more out of place. I gasped in disbelief as it occurred to me; it wasn't in the same place. It was closer, much closer.

I squinted and made out disheveled grey hair and a black hat. Looking down, I saw that her white legs were exposed under the coat. The skin looked pallid and cold. Out in the frigid cold there was a woman, dressed entirely in black, standing behind a tree, and facing the village. I did not know what to do, she seemed delirious, but at the same time her fiendish whispering was unsettling. Her hands were hidden in the sleeves of her expensive-looking coat that looked fit for a summer funeral. I couldn't tell what her hands were holding from where I was standing, behind her and up the hill. She was facing the village and mumbling the same morbid words, on repeat with her hoarse whisper like a curse. "Death begets death... run.... hide ..... No good... You will be found.... All in time... Time.... Time...Time...."

She filled me with dread, but I had to walk past her to get to the bridge and the village. My only alternative was to stand there and pray she never turned around and die in the cold waiting. Between us there were a few well rounded trees and yards of snow about a foot deep. It was impossible to be silent with the snow, but she had ignored me thus far. Despite the shaking in my arms, I willed myself down the slope, inch by inch, never removing my eyes from her. There was an energy of malevolence radiating from her, I felt nauseous from the pressure of it as I grew closer.

I slowly passed her from a distance as I continued downhill. Soon I was far enough down the slope to look up and see her face. Curiosity got the better of me and looked back up the hill. I stifled a scream by shoving the side of my hand into my mouth and biting down painfully. Her face was ghastly white, aged with deep running wrinkles, but it was her eyes most of all that made me want to scream. In the darkness, it looked like her eye shadow was blood and her eye sockets were hollow black holes. She was facing the village, looking upon that village as a wolf would look upon a herd of sheep before a slaughter.

I was frozen once more in fear, hoping, and praying that she would not see me, hoping that her eye sockets were indeed hollow. Then it occurred to me, contrary to her seeming age, she saw well enough to bring herself up this hill in this monstrous weather. With that realization, it was time for me to leave, to distance myself from this chilling woman dressed in all black. I raised my right foot out of the snow and gently stepped back. The ball of my foot near soundlessly pushed against the hard snow and the heel of my foot began to settle down. I felt a hard contact under my heel, assuming it to be a rock, I kept pushing down. A loud crack erupted from the branch as it snapped under my weight.

The woman stopped whispering and her head shook as she turned her head to face me. It was like she was having tremors. The snow clung to her hat and hair, making her resemble a spectral figure from a nightmare. Bathed in moonlight, her skin looked as pale as death. As my eyes met with hers, a shiver ran down my neck. Her eyes were glazed over and completely void of the characteristics of life. Those eyes looked like the vacant gaze of a reanimated corpse without a soul.

A violent surge of repulsion overtook me and an intense desire for life overtook me. I wanted to tear those eyes out, I did not want this thing to see me.

"What are you!?" I bellowed into the night, my voice echoing through the silent woods.

It did not flinch, did not blink, did not answer. It continued to stare at me with those glazed over, lifeless eyes. My eyes felt dry from staring at it through the darkness. I blinked nervously, hoping and praying that when I opened my eyes she would be gone. Nothing more than a nightmare. The paranoid thought raced through my head that if I blink, then she would appear just inches of my face. My heart was beating painfully like a drum telling of impending danger.

The silence lingered, neither of us moving, and a sudden pang of hunger made me feel meek. My mind was starting to fall off its hinges with all the racing thoughts and exhaustion. The weight of exhaustion made my eyes feel so incredibly heavy. They burned as I struggled to keep them open. My eye lids fell shut and I felt my body becoming numb as sleep overtook me and my body collapsed.

My mind shifted back to a memory, but I couldn't remember if this was an old or new memory. I was pulling up to my house after a long shift at the courthouse. It was a full moon, and the only lights were the lights inside the house coming from the first-floor windows and the light inside my car. A scream pierced the night, propelling me into action. I didn't know what was happening, but I knew had to hurry. I slammed the door shut and sprinted up my walkway and past the snow-covered garden. The front door was left a jar, and the doorknob was scraped all around the keyhole, as if by a knife. I put my hand on the knob and thrust the door open.

Fear jolted me back to consciousness as I remembered the woman's ghastly face against the fog of my failing mind. I could see her, standing still, at the same spot, staring down upon me. I felt a horrible falling sensation. I had lost consciousness a moment too long. In my numbness, I had begun to fall backward, down the hill. My body was being berated by the impact of rolling down the hill, colliding with rocks and grazing a tree on my way down. The impact woke me fully from my sleep. I threw out my hands to grab onto something, but there was nothing but cold air, mocking my desperate attempts. The next roll ended with a rock to the back of my head which plunged me into an abyss of darkness. Sound, sensation, everything flickered out in an instant...

~ II ~

INTO THE VOID

I felt the cold everywhere. I smelled damp dirt. The air was dry against my nostrils and burning from the cold. My world was only darkness. Thoughts raced through my head as I struggled to connect the different sensations I felt. Where was I? Was I dead? Is my afterlife an infinity of cold and loneliness?

The numbness of my nose and ears burned as if they were submerged in a cold fire. As I turned my head, a cold wetness grazed my cheek. Still, I could see nothing but darkness. My right hand felt stiff as if it was encased in ice. I winced in pain as I forced my fingers together to form a clenched fist. It was the first realization that I was alive. A raspy cough escaped my dry throat, breaking the silence around me. I gradually opened my eyes, realizing I could see again. The world I was greeted with was still shrouded in darkness, but I could see white as well.

I sat up with my legs laid out ahead of me and looked around. A world painted in white surrounded me and confusion clouded my thoughts. Nothing made sense in that frozen hell. It took me a few minutes to remember where I was. "I'm alive? I'm.... Alive." I said it with more confidence in a coarse voice. It seemed unbelievable that I survived the fall and the cold.

I looked up above me and wondered how I was still alive. Dusk was settling in; the sky was littered with thick white clouds that were barely visible against the dark grey sky. Over the horizon was the last sliver of beautiful magenta light, retreating out toward the west. The world around me was beautiful like the world inside a snow globe. For a moment I sat in awe at it all, enjoying the start of the sunset. If only she were here with me to enjoy this too. She always loved sunsets; she'd call me up from my desk just to run to the nearest window to enjoy it together. The memories felt so far away as I sat in the snow, but there was no time to dwell on that.

I pushed myself up from my knees and onto my feet. Weakness flooded my body and my back felt stiff. I twisted my waist to the left and right and felt a satisfying crack under my coat. It felt relieving, but it did not cure the weakness in the rest of my body. I took a deep breath of the cold crisp air, filling my lungs with the piercing dry air. I exhaled slowly, regaining composure. Out ahead of me, I saw a bridge illuminated by streetlamps, devoid of tire tracks. Of course, in this blizzard, any tire tracks would be immediately covered anyway. It was a short metal bridge over a coursing river. I could see some collections of ice on the edges of the riverbed where the bushes reached out.

I slowly limped to the nearest streetlamp. Under that fluorescent light, I could feel some relief as my memories flooded back into my mind and I could remember it all. For some reason that I could not perceive, I was still alive. Behind me there was a hill. It was the same hill with the whispering woman in black. I scanned the trees with my eyes and no matter where I looked, there was no sign of her. There were no tracks either, just the indents from me rolling down the hill. Maybe she was just a figment of my imagination. A paranoid feeling compelled me to keep looking but the sun was still setting, and I was still a long way out from the village on foot. I pulled my gaze away from the hill and back toward the bridge. I crossed the two-lane street with scarcely a look to either side. There was no one coming and no one going. The whole day, I was the only one crazy enough to be on the road in a blizzard like this. The people of this village knew better.

I began to cross the bridge on foot. The village on the other side seemed like a sanctuary, illuminated by warm and welcoming lights from the windows and billowing smoke from the chimneys. I began to cough from my parched throat; the feeling of exhaustion was becoming too intense to handle. My eyes rolled in their sockets. I could barely focus.

My boots stabbed into the snow without grace as I stumbled across the bridge, drunk with exhaustion. The howls of the wind were my only company on that bridge. As the bridge gently buckled from the intense wind, I had to grab onto the metal railing to steady myself.

The light from the village was a beautiful shade of yellow, like sunlight at the end of a long dark tunnel. My vision was fading with my strength. The edges of my sight were going dark until I could only see straight in front of me.

I drifted back into another far-off memory as my vision continued to narrow. This time I was an eight-year-old child seeking solace under my bed sheets, hoping my father would come and rescue me from despair as I bawled my eyes out. He came into my room and flicked on the lights and saw me balled up in my bed under the sheets. I could hear a long sigh over the sound of my stifled sniffles and tears. I felt relief knowing my father was there. He always knew what to do, or what to say depending on the situation.

My laundry was in a pile at the foot of my bed, my book bag was left open, and the remainder of my peanut butter sandwich was hanging off the edge of the main pocket. The walls had posters of superheroes and one especially imposing poster of a tiger on the prowl above my bed. My father shook his brown mane with disapproval. The sides of his hair and his well-kept beard were streaked with silver, not quite white yet. He bent over to pick up the remainder of my school lunch.

"Son, it's...." He wanted to say it's alright, but he knew it would be a lie. Instead, he sighed and corrected himself, speaking with a heavy heart. "It's been hard on everyone, but we'll visit her from time to time. She's not dead yet and even then, we'll always have our memories of how she was." I was still weeping uncontrollably; my face was soaked with tears. My father brushed back his hair with a hand and scratched his beard in thought. With his deep-set voice, he asked, "What was your first memory of grandma?" I finally withdrew my head from under the blanket, looking up at him as I thought. His eyes looked tired, but he was not physically exhausted. His mother was suffering from Alzheimer's disease. He had recently decided to put her in a "home." He felt very guilty about it, but he knew that he had no other choice; she was too much for just the family to handle. She was becoming more confused and physically aggressive. It was heartbreaking to see my kind grandmother losing everything that made her herself because of some terrible disease without a cure.

After a few minutes of thoughtful consideration, I recounted a lazy midsummer day. She was trying to sleep, but I wanted a story, so she told me the three little pigs. It was the first thing I remembered of her and one of my favorite memories. "Dad, why did we have to put her in a home? I love grandma, she'll get better, won't she? It'll just take a while since she's really old right?"

My father stretched the tight muscles in his neck and turned to give me a somber look with downcast eyes. He furrowed his thick eyebrows and put his hand on my young bony shoulder. "Sometimes, things can't be fixed son. Grandma has a sickness of the brain that only gets worse, it doesn't get better. Do you understand?" he asked. The creases in his face were more apparent as the pain spread across his eyes, his forehead, and his lips. It was the first time I looked deeply into my father's face; he was growing older too. I nodded, not really understanding at the time, but accepting that my father understood. "You can't save everyone," he said with down crested shoulders.

I took a breath as I leaned against the railing, my mind back in the present. Looking over the railing and into the river, all I could see was a void of nothingness. "You can't save everyone," my father's words echoed in mind as if they wanted to remind me of something I wasn't supposed to forget. There was a memory deep in the back of my mind that I couldn't reach although I could feel it itching. Like it wanted to escape but was trapped, muddled by my cold and hunger.

There were scattered glimmers of silver as the moonlight hit the surface of the churning river. All signs of the day were now long gone. I could feel the waves gently moving the bridge. I heard the scurrying of small feet nearby and I immediately looked up, across the bridge. There was a streetlamp at the end of the bridge. Its light caught the tail of a black cat. Although these little devils are associated with bad luck, it felt good to see another living thing other than the glossy eyed hag in the woods. The night didn't feel as alone after seeing the cat.

I mustered up the strength to keep moving forward, leaning on the frigid railing as I walked. I reached the streetlamp at last. I inhaled deeply, but I could no longer smell anything. The fall must have messed me up worse than I thought. In the dead of night, I heard the hoarse whisper of a woman's voice so clearly that it seemed to come from my own thoughts. "You are *alone...* You will die *alone.*"

My heart skipped a beat as I whirled around to find the source of the voice. There was no one there except for me. The street was deserted and no one was on the bridge. Loneliness bore its claws into me, but deep inside I still felt warm enough to go on. I knew that I was not alone. I loved and was loved too deeply to ever be alone.

"You're wrong..." I gasped for air, but I felt that I had to answer the claims of the wind. "I am never... alone! My sweet Annabel is ...." I couldn't finish the sentence, it felt like the words got caught in my throat and almost choked me. She wasn't here with me in this forsaken weather. I continued into the village silently. The momentary feeling of defiance faded and was carried off with the wind.

The first few buildings in the village seemed like old-fashioned stores. From under the snow, I made out a sign reading, "John White's Shoe Masonry." My plan was to knock on the door of the first house I saw that seemed to have moving people inside of it. The first block of stores were all empty. Some had dim lights on. I walked closer to a TV store which still had the fat backed TVs from the nineties. As I grew closer to it, the sound of static grew louder. I looked inside and saw a disheveled store, as if it had been recently vandalized. More than half of the TVs were either shattered and left on the ground or shattered on the shelves. There were a few TV sets still working that showed white static with the irritating buzzing set to maximum volume. I backed away and continued down the street.

I nervously looked behind my shoulder with every few steps I took, half expecting to see the old hag following me. I reached a large intersection and saw a deserted gas station to the right.

There seemed to be a truck parked in front of the convenience store there. There seemed to be a light on in the convenience store. I decided to investigate the gas station.

Once I reached it, I realized none of the four gas kiosks had a light on. The light in the minimart appeared to have gone off as well. It seemed like another dead end. There was nothing there, so I began to walk away until a flicker of light caught the corner of my eye. As I turned toward it, I noticed something had moved swiftly by me. I turned to look back toward the gas station, but now the convenience store's light was on, along with half of the gas kiosks. The bright lights stung my eyes and I squinted to see. It was eerie to say the least, I did not notice anyone go into the store or hear a door, but I was desperate and compelled to find a break from my loneliness.

With every step toward the convenience store, the razor-sharp wind slashed and bit at my face, trying to keep me away from whoever was there, but I did not heed nature's warnings. A black cat, somehow familiar, wisped through my legs as it ran in the opposite direction. If crossing a black cat's path is bad luck, what does it mean to be going in the opposite direction? Perhaps my luck was even worse than the cat's.

The light in the store was a fluorescent white, making everything inside the store look pale and sickly like a morgue. I looked through the frost-bitten glass and saw a rather ordinary gas station store. The light cast a poor light on the pallid food, making it seem old and unused with layers of dust upon them. I scanned the small room crowded with goods but found no one there.

There was an unsettling feeling in my stomach that was not simple hunger. It felt like a sense of doom or anxiety that was gnawing at me from the inside. I could not fathom how or why the lights turned on, surely someone was in there. Looking down at the floor, I saw bags of chips and other snack foods torn open with their contents littering the unkempt floor. The more I peered through the glass, the more the signs of neglect became apparent to me. It was not the lighting that made this place look sinister, but something else entirely. The floors looked like they were streaked with mud and dirt.

Shaky at first, then firm, my hand went for the ice-cold metal handle. The contact gave me a chill as my fingers wrapped around its dry surface. Somewhere outside of my line of vision, a door slammed shut. The sudden sound terrified me. I heard something crawling on many legs- piercing the snow, tapping against the concrete in rapid succession. It went further away, then closer, and then closer still. Thankfully though, whatever it was sounded like it was on the other side of the door and not outside with me.

As my eyes darted to the right, I noticed a dark room behind the register. Inside that room was a counter and I couldn't believe what was lying there. I squinted and pulled my face toward the glass to check again. I caught a glimpse of a man's legs on the counter in the dark room, laying there without a torso. I audibly gasped and pulled my hand back from the door handle. It looked more like chopped meat than the legs of a man. He was wearing thick jeans before he lost his legs, whoever the sorry soul was. The fibers of meat stuck out from the pants, dry brown fibers without blood as if they were out in the cold for days. If there were no jeans attached, I could have easily mistaken it for any other animal. The thought made me sick to my stomach from the abject horror.

My head was spinning, and my breathing became rapid and shallow. "What the hell is going on here?" I wondered out loud. Fear made me hyper vigilant, wondering what would have done that to a person, tearing off a leg... and where was the rest... of him? The thought made my stomach jump into my throat.

I scanned the remainder of that dark room. My eyes found nothing in that darkness save for two speckles of red light staring at me. Maybe eyes? I couldn't tell but a feeling in my gut told me I shouldn't stick around to find out. I turned and began to walk away from the gas station, following the black cat's path. The cat was running from something; it was smarter than I was. I stopped at the first gas kiosk to try to collect myself and slow my breathing. I leaned my hand against the corner of the kiosk and on the other side where I could not see, I felt a soft fabric brush against my left hand.

It felt like the fabric of a woman's coat. I froze in place thinking what it could be. I couldn't remember seeing anyone else at the gas station. The lights were out before I had come by. Was it another villager?

The sound of a rasping breath beside me gave me a feeling of dread before I could even turn my head. Then I saw *it* again. The white skin, the black coat. It was her again. The lights overhead flickered off. I couldn't contain it, I screamed, running away from this occult stalker. The hunger and the exhaustion completely left my mind, in its place was a primal sense of danger and a flight reaction. There were times in my life where I would stay and fight, but everything about this alarmed in my head that it was time to run. The reaction was instantaneous.

I kept running without looking back until I passed a few intersections down the road, I noticed the beginning of a residential area. I stopped running, panting from exhaustion. As I began to steady myself, I listened closely to the night air. There were no footsteps or ticking of spider legs to be heard. I breathed a sigh of relief as I calmly walked down the street and observed the modest two-story houses stretching down the road to the left and right. A few houses had a warm yellow glow coming out of their windows, but most were completely dark. Some of the dark houses had strange symbols on the door. The symbols were disconcerting, some seemed to resemble an inverted cross and another looked like a man riding the wings of an eagle. I looked down at the leather-bound sports watch on my left wrist, but I couldn't read the time in the dark. I pressed down on the night light button on the side of the watch. The watch glowed green and bore the numbers 9:43. I couldn't believe it; I must have been walking the streets for hours now.

"It's a bit early for people to be asleep," I thought to myself. I felt uneasy walking down the deserted streets at night. I kept looking behind my shoulder to make sure that crazy woman was not following me. What was she? A demon, a witch, or simply deranged. I couldn't shake the paranoid feeling that there were still eyes watching me.

I kept walking down the road, nervously looking back after every few steps, until I reached the intersection of Samael Avenue and Arcane Road. I looked down Arcane Road. There seemed to be more lit houses on my right, so I chose to go right. The first house to my left, after taking the right, was dark, but the next one was brightly lit.

There was a full aluminum trash can in front of the dark house. The snow on top of the trash can looked pink, and I could just barely make out a handle to something narrow and wooden with black wrappings at the base. I saw a swift shadow run through my peripheral vision as I passed the abandoned house. I peered at the dark house, but there was nothing there. The blinds of the windows were tightly drawn. I listened for the source of the motion, but all I could hear was my own breathing and the gentle whistling of the wind.

I waited a moment longer and I heard some kind of coughing scream as if something could barely get the breath out to scream. The sound raised the hairs on the back of my neck. It was a horrid noise, as if a cat was being gutted alive. I stood stalk still and listened carefully. The night was only getting worse, and my adrenaline could only carry me so far until my body gives out.

I heard the noise a few more times, a gurgle like the source was choking on water, and then silence. The silence was followed by a barely audible gnawing sound. It sounded like something was chewing on a tough piece of steak. Listening carefully, I could trace the sound to behind the dark house. There was a horrible hiss from a cat, like a dyeing breath, and this was followed by a tearing sound. My heart dropped and my body began to shake. I tasted a harsh bitterness in my mouth again as my body trembled uncontrollably. It felt like I would pass out at any minute.

The creature behind the house began to drag its prey out from behind the house. Again, my breathing became more shallow and rapid. My eyes were darting around like a frantic mouse trying to find a proper place to hide from an oncoming owl. I recalled the handle in the trash can, hopefully it was a hammer. I swooped down and pulled an icy bat out of the trash for assurance as I began to sneak toward the neighboring well-lit house. Half of the wooden bat had splintered off, and its tip was distinctly red. I tried to ignore that as I raised the bat, ready to strike when needed.

The streetlamp for the block was off, probably damaged by the storm. I carefully inched toward the neighboring house, trying my best to avoid falling. My eyes were fixed at the back corner of the dark house. I saw a long, thin tail. It reminded me of a moving piece of rope. The creature seemed to have black fur; I could barely make it out against the darkness. It had a long snout that held a limp black cat by its neck.

It twitched its nose and released the dead cat. Dark, viscous blood dripped from its mouth, and flowed out of the black cat's neck. It reared its ugly head and stood on two feet as it sniffed the air in my direction. It was a giant rat, easily five feet, akin to a beaver more so than a rat except for its sharp fangs. It was a behemoth of a rat that defied all logic. The largest rats on record are Gambian Pouched rats and those can only grow to three feet, but they could never be as large or as strong as this monstrosity.

My gloved hand tightened around the baseball bat's hard handle. It was heavy in my weary arms. The rat hissed and arched its back upward as it prepared to pounce at me. Fear told me to run, but a distant memory told me to stand my ground and "handle it." With a great effort, I raised the bat and readied to swing it. My arms burned as I held the bat above my waist, but I stood rooted to the spot. I stood not by fear, but by a determination to survive. I could feel someone else holding me up as if I wasn't alone. It felt like a familiar and warm hand.

I was reminded of the times I couldn't run from life's trials. I was in my twenties, holding onto my umbrella so tightly that my hands began to hurt. There was light rain on a gloomy autumn day. The sky was as grey as the cold slab of rock in the ground before me. The slab read "Here lies Jonathan Aman: Beloved husband and father." The tombstone had an engraving of an old tree on it, requested by my father. I clenched my teeth and breathed deeply, holding back tears. The one thing I could not hold back though was my guilt. I was overcome by grief as I fell to my knees before the tombstone in the rain. "I'm sorry. I'm sorry for everything. I'm sorry I couldn't be there for you! Now it's too late," I sobbed to myself.

I couldn't breathe, I felt like a hand had wrapped around my gut and it was squeezing the life out of my lungs. There were dozens of people here for my father's funeral, but I felt like an island, alone in the middle of an endless sea.

A gentle hand touched my shoulder, followed by a gentle pair of lips that kissed my lips. I could breathe again. I closed my eyes and rested my cheek against her soft hand. "It's alright James," she whispered into my ear. Annabel rested her jaw on my shoulder and gently kissed my cheek. "He's not gone. As long as you carry his memory inside of you, he's not gone completely."

I turned and our eyes locked. Both of our eyes were filled with tears. They were my own words, thrown right back at me. After all these years, she remembered what I had forgotten. She was the one who gave me strength to stand again.

The memory filled my body with enough strength to face my fears. I stretched my biceps as I held the bat. My heartbeat had a new vigor as the rat began to gallop toward me. I swung with all my force and broke off the remaining chunk of the bat against its ugly face. The beast was incredibly heavy, but I swung with enough force to send it rolling away. Its left eye was crushed and bleeding after the impact. Its bright red blood mixed with the dark blood of the cat matting its short fur. It grunted in pain, and slowly got back onto its feet.

The exertion was too much for my haggard body and there wasn't much left of the bat either. I felt my blood sugar drop dramatically. As the dizzy beast tried to steady itself, I decided that the wise choice was to escape before I have a furious rat to deal with instead of a hungry rat. I turned and staggered down the road, still clutching the fragmented bat.

The neighboring house's lights were on. I banged on the archaic door with my left hand. Just above my hand, on the door, was a knocker that resembled an old-fashioned balance. One side of the scale was engulfed in fire.

The door was slowly opened by a smiling man with a bovine look in his eyes. His light brown hair was combed to the side with some grey on his temples. He was cleanly shaved and wore a very cozy brown sweater with a checkered design. He seemed friendly enough, thankfully. I needed a friend to help me survive this night.

I was honest with him, "I need to come in now! There's some rabid rat out here and I haven't eaten a proper meal in a couple days. Please, help me!" I exclaimed with desperation.

He looked me up and down. His eyes settled upon the bat in my hands. "No weapons in this house sir." I threw the bat behind the bushes in front of his house. "Please come in!" he said as he stepped aside and swung the door wide open for me. I quickly stepped in and he closed the door behind me, calmly, given the fact that the unknown guest at his door had just been holding a broken bat. There was a thud against the door followed by forceful scratching. The monster was not giving up its pursuit so easily. It was trying to dig its nails into the door as hard as it could.

I looked over to my amiable host with concern. He still wore the same smile; he was completely unfazed by the scratching at the door. For a moment, I thought perhaps the sound was a figment of my imagination until I heard another thump. "What do we do about that thing?" I asked. I was cock eyed from exhaustion, fading as I struggled to stay upright.

He looked at me and said, "It will go away, everything goes away." I was taken aback by such a morbid statement from this stranger, but its truth stung me. I felt heavy with pain. "You look far too thin! Let's fatten you up!" exclaimed my strange host as he started walking toward his kitchen.

I automatically followed, without much thought. I noticed a simple couch out of the corner of my eye and some scattered lights on the ceiling. There was no fireplace. The floor I walked on was hardwood and clean. The small house had a cozy feel, but there was a strange smell in the air. It reminded me of spoiled eggs, but it was masked by the scent of vanilla.

He seated me on a cushioned wooden chair. His table was dark oak and had no tablecloth. The top of the table was littered with specks of dark red and some smeared black stains. It felt clean enough to the touch though. His wife was washing the dishes in the sink from a seemingly messy dinner. The plates were covered with a thick brown gelatin-like sauce. It looked disgusting; I hoped what they planned to offer me would be better.

She was not a particularly attractive woman. Her features were mostly flat and of little consequence; her black hair was not bold, but dull. The deep violet blouse she wore would have looked beautiful on another woman, but on her it looked like any other piece of clothing, it may as well have been a dull shade of grey. She was a dowdy woman, and she wore the same naive look of stupid glee as her husband. They were both senselessly happy and carefree during this nightmarish blizzard in an eerie village. Even sitting in their kitchen with the sound of the running faucet, I could still clearly hear the whistles of the wind and violent shaking of the trees outside.

He whispered into his wife's ear, and she slowly nodded and turned off the faucet. She walked over to their white refrigerator. The refrigerator had speckles of yellow from its years of age. As she opened the bottom compartment of the refrigerator, I gasped. It was full of red meat covered in fat white maggots. They borrowed into and out of the meat and wriggled all over the pounds and pounds of bloody meat in the freezer.

I closed my eyes tightly and rubbed them, hoping to remove the layer of falsity induced by exhaustion from my eyes. When I opened them again, the maggots were gone, but the refrigerator was still stocked to the brim with red meat. She removed a particularly large cut of the meat; it looked like a steak. My mouth began to water. It seemed as if my dreams would come true.

As she thawed the meat, she placed some bread and cheese in front of me, and I hungrily consumed these meager appetizers. "Thank you so much for your generosity!" I exclaimed with a half full mouth. The butter was unsalted, and the bread was dry but edible. "Where is your salt?" I asked.

Her smile faltered for a moment but came back immediately. "There is no salt in this household... You were just what we were looking for! Please, have some coffee, it's a special brew," she said in an airy voice. "You'll love the secret ingredient, but I'll never tell!" She gave me an awkward wink. I felt uncomfortable as I reached for the plain white mug of coffee, but I knew I could certainly use a pick me up.

She had begun to fry the steak on a hot pan over her stove as I took a gulp of the hot coffee. The steak gave a putrid odor; it was not quite right. It smelled like spoiled eggs. I took a couple more gulps of the coffee. It tasted like dirt; it was probably the worst cup of coffee I ever had.

"Thanks for the great cup of Joe miss!" I lied to be polite. She turned her attention from the steak on the pan and began to simply stare at me. The smile was still glued to her plain, pale face. Her vapid eyes were fixated on me. What was she waiting for?

I took a deep breath and yawned. I felt a sudden surge of drowsiness. My eyes began to flicker. Peering into the black cup of coffee, I noticed a swirl of blue in the cup. My eyes shot upwards for a moment. Just long enough to catch a glimpse of her face contorting into a wider wicked smile that showed her crooked yellowing teeth. She was slowly walking toward me with a look of anticipation.

I put my palms on the tabletop and pushed to get up, but it was too late. My muscles were going numb and as I pushed, all I could do was push my chair backward and fall onto the back of my skull.

My world became black, and much colder. My face was covered in something wet and cold. I rolled over and opened my eyes. I saw a black sky void of stars. It seemed that I was lying motionless in the snow. I turned my head side to side, but I couldn't see anything except trees covered in snow in either direction. I began to cough and again my world became darkness.

~ III ~

OUT OF THE FRYING PAN

"Annabel, I don't think I can do it anymore. I'm just... too tired. I'm going to drop out of law school," I concluded.

She raised her left eyebrow at me then smiled and shook her head. She rolled over and put her hand on my shoulder sympathetically. "I know it's hard, but I know you. I know you would never forgive yourself if you gave up now. You can do this, and I'm not just saying that because I love you. I'm saying it because it's true." She gently kissed me on the cheek. She had just graduated from medical school. I was always there for her then and now that I needed her, she was there for me too. "We'll get through this together just like everything else." My throat started to feel tight as I remembered the 'everything else.'

We started dating in high school and were long distance while we were in college, but we made it work. It wasn't all just a perfect relationship either. We had our fights and times when we wouldn't talk to each other for weeks. That's the trouble with starting young, there was still so much growing to do. I'm always so thankful we never had to grow apart; we always found a way to grow intertwined, supporting each other through losses, wins, and everything in between.

I embraced her as my tears started to fall. "Thank you, I needed to hear that. We'll make it through this just like everything else." I withdrew from her shoulder to look at her entrancing green eyes. "I love you; you know that?" I asked with a chuckle. It was such a relief to be finally living with her after so many years apart for college.

"Right back at you, you goof! What would you do without me?" she asked with a mocking shake of her head. "Now it's time to get up and out of bed alright?" I felt so tired, I just laid there in bed. "Come on! It's time to get up, get up James!" Her voice suddenly picked up in pitch and seemed to hold a tone of panic, "Get up now James! You're running out of time!" she shouted with urgency. The shout was so loud my head jerked and suddenly I realized my eyes were closed. I was asleep. She shouted again in my ear and pulled me abruptly from a deep sleep...

I awoke feeling groggy and with a strange itching sensation around my wrists. There was something heavy scraping against the floor above me like it was being dragged on a hardwood floor. I opened my eyes and peered through the dim lighting. I appeared to be in some morbid basement. It was lit by the light of a few scattered candles. To my right was a sturdy table covered in dark red blood. My heart sank and I tried to move my arms only to realize they were bound by rough scratchy rope. I felt helpless as I awaited the hunter, trapped like a rabbit in a snare, hanging by my arms. The table had a butcher's knife stuck in its wooden surface, awaiting further use presumably. Ahead of me there was a long staircase that led up to a door outlined by white light.

With a feeling of dread, I continued to survey my bleak surroundings. What I saw to my left made me gasp so violently that I hurt my throat. I began to tug desperately until the rope dug painfully into my wrists and subdued my initial panic and any hope of surviving.

I hung there, wide eyed, staring at the limp arm hanging to my left. There was an immense puddle of blood under the hanging arm. The cut had apparently been clean; the white bone jutting obscenely out of the flesh bore no cracks, only a clean surgical cut. The surrounding brick red meat resembled a cow's thigh. The blood was still dripping from it, but very slowly and a maroon red. The puddle underneath looked thick and sticky, like most of the blood had already coagulated.

I tried to remember where I was before I fell asleep and got tied up. There was a pause upstairs and a coarse cough. Think... Think... Where am I? I closed my eyes tight but the tighter I closed them, the more vivid the vision of black sky with sprinkles of snow on my face became. I kept my eyes closed and looked right and left, I was lying on my back in the snow. To the right I saw a bridge. I opened my eyes again and I was back in the dungeon. Now the memories were coming back, I was lost in a blizzard and came to this village seeking shelter. My hosts must have poisoned the coffee I was drinking, and I am probably in their basement. The realization gave me a small victory, but it was short lived as I heard the footsteps upstairs resume.

I looked up at the rope entrapping my hands. The rope looked old, as if it had been reused many times over. I grasped the rope and began to tug on the knots with little success. The scraping upstairs was just over my head and progressing toward the door ahead of me. Soon, the cannibal would be upon me as I hung helplessly. As I tried to undo the knot, I looked around for an alternative exit. The candlelight was not bright enough to see the entire perimeter of the basement. I couldn't see any doors except for the one leading upstairs, which would take me straight into the path of an armed psycho.

I began to hear hysterical laughter upstairs. The scraping slowed for a moment as the fiend had a fit of laughter where he pounded his fist against the wall. It shook the building's meek frame and some dust from the ceiling fell into my hair. After a frantic effort, the knot was still too stubborn, so I began to gnaw at the ropes. I dug in with my teeth through the rope like a desperate rat. The sharp strands went in-between my teeth and pierced my gums painfully as I struggled to save myself. I wanted to scream from the pain, but my instinct to survive pushed through the pain.

The footsteps upstairs continued, and my heart began to race as blood began to run down my gums and mouth. I could feel the old rope tearing as I scraped away the layers of thread with my teeth. The scraping was now right beside the door. I pulled my hands apart as hard as I could, and the weakened rope unraveled. It was just in front of the door now. The knob was turning slowly. My mind raced. My head twisted from the left to the right. I was determined to find a place to hide.

I blew out the candles at the foot of the stairs, and around the table to my right. I pulled the butcher's knife out of the table, yanking it out of the wood with great effort. Before the doorknob turned, I was hidden under the table. My knees were soaked with a cool and thick fluid. I struggled to push out the thoughts of the bleeding man or woman from my head. That poor person's pain must have been horrifying, but I had no time to ponder the rivers of hell under my feet, nor time to feel remorse for the lost souls before me who had trodden the same ground in hopes of haven.

The door creaked open and a few profanities were uttered under my not so hospitable host's breath. He slowly descended the stairs, there was no longer a scraping noise following him, but that only made me cling to my knife tighter. The stairs moaned with agony under my host's weight.

Once he reached the foot of the stairs, a candle on the far side of the room, by the hanging arm, illuminated my pursuer's face in an orange glow. He peered into the darkness with a strained smile that was more akin to a grimace; he bore his teeth like an animal on the prowl. His face looked warped. A faint glint directed my eyes toward his waist. He was holding a grandiose axe. Its blade was larger than the seat of a chair. The axe seemed heavy; its smiling holder was perspiring from the effort of keeping the axe at waist level. An axe like that would probably make a clean cut through a cow, never mind a person. The margin for error was tight. If I messed up for a second, he would probably cleave that axe through me like a hot knife through butter.

I held my breath and tried not to move, despite an uncontrollable shivering. Adrenaline kept me focused on survival and pushed the fear out of my mind. "Where are you hiding neighbor? I have a present for you," he hissed through tight lips as he struggled against the weight of the axe. His eyes still bore the same vacant look even through his straining hunt. The more I looked at his face in the dark, the less humanity I could find in it. It looked more like a mask. I could feel his hostility in the air, but his face didn't express any of it.

He began to slowly step toward the table. I bit my bottom lip as I braced myself to swing the knife. My mouth was filled with an iron taste from my bleeding gums, made worse as my front teeth pierced my chapped lips. I began to think about what was next. If I survived my encounter with this deranged cannibal, I would have to go out and face the fierce elements again. A lose, lose situation, but as long as I am still breathing, there is hope. "Hope for what?" asked a small voice in my head. I ignored it and resolved to fight for my life and if I won, then I would stop this monster from terrorizing other victims too.

He stopped, facing the table, and slowly lifted his axe up above his head with a great effort. My heart began to race as I instinctually shot through from under just as the axe shredded through the thick table. The wood splintered and crackled from the axe's awesome power. Its blade pierced deep into the concrete floor. Dust filled the air from the shattered concrete.

I shielded my eyes with my hand and looked up at my adversary. I quickly stood erect and swung the knife into his back. I missed his spine, but I pierced his flesh deep enough to hit an organ, probably a kidney from what I could remember from Annabel's medical books. The monster let out a squeal like a wounded boar. I felt an odd satisfaction from his pain, knowing he must have caused far worse pain to his many victims throughout the years. My relief was shortly lived, the wounded boar threw an elbow into my side, sending a jolt of pain through my body. He was not giving up so easily, but neither would I.

Looking up, I saw the golden lining of light around the door, my route to freedom. I sprinted toward the doorstep. I was up the first two steps until a hand slapped my left ankle. I flailed my arms out and clasped my hands onto a stair just in time to stop my face from bouncing against the splintered wooden edge. I felt a piece of wood slide deep into my left hand. I winced from the pain, but quickly scrambled to my feet.

My aggressor's hand gripped my ankle tightly, trying to crush my ankle with superhuman strength. I heard some strange shuffling upstairs, like some clumsy drunk was running around in circles. I grabbed onto the railing and tried to pull my leg free, but he was stronger and began to drag me down the stairs as he grunted like a dying animal. I thrust my free leg into his face;

I felt his nose snap under my boot's heel. His grip immediately loosened, and I flew up the stairs on all fours.

I threw the door open and looked around the dark living room. The whole house was morphed into some satanic ritual site lit only by yellow wax candles scattered across the floor. I could scarcely see the walls; everything outside of the candles' limited light was hidden behind a black veil of darkness. I could hear some creature crawling on all fours on the other side of the veil. Its steps were heavier than even the rat I had encountered before.

My heart dropped as I heard something clambering up the steps behind me with a snapping sound as it came. I turned around to see my prior host looking at me with his head hanging upside down. The rest of his twisted and demented body crawled up the stairs on all fours with his chest facing upwards. The cracking was from its joints that were twisted against what was natural. His mouth was open, still wearing a grotesque smile. It was no longer a human smile; he was the perversion of humanity, a demon. I slammed the door in its face and heard him rolling down the stairs. I hoped that cannibal would simply die.

I looked closely at the doorknob; it still had the key in its lock. I turned the key and immediately pulled it out and threw it across the dimly lit room. Something began to shuffle in the dark unknown of the house. My eyes found no weapon this time. I began to inch across the room toward the main door to escape this madhouse. I stayed in the dim light of the wavering candles so I could see anything that came to attack me, and at least see my own way to freedom too.

I felt the weight of eyes staring at me from the shadows. The candles left an eerie glare on one of the windows. I peered into it, trying to see what the other side held for me.

The moment briefly reminded me of something Annabel told me years ago. "No one really knows what the other side holds, but it can't be so terrible. It's probably beautiful there! As beautiful as your mind can conceive," said Annabel. Her smile once again reassured me. How could I doubt such an angelic face? Her eyes filled my cold heart with warmth.

"Humph, it would be nice if one could choose when they go," I retorted as I wrapped my arms around her small shoulders. I wanted to live as long as she lived, but not a moment longer. I wanted to be with her in this world, and the next. I loved her amazing spirit; there was an incredible fire in her heart that made every moment with her sublime. Even when that feisty spirit was yelling at me. "I would hate to linger in this life without you."

"It's not our choice when the reaper comes. It comes for us all when the time is right. It's just how life is," her eyes suddenly lost their sense of playfulness, replaced by a thousand-yard stare; lost in a deep thought. Her gentle hands wrapped around mine and squeezed as she nuzzled her cheek against my chest. "Promise me that whatever happens, that you will look for me on the other side. Promise me, that you will always love me, but more importantly... Promise me you will keep living and enjoy your life until that time comes when we meet again, whenever it's meant to be," she whispered softly.

I brought my lips to her ear and gently whispered back, "I promise. No matter where you go, I will find you. If you are atop the tallest, most beautiful mountain in heaven, I will climb it without rest to find you even if the angels try to chain me to the ground. Nothing will keep me from you, my love."

Death was following my every step for the last two days. Only God knows when Death will strike me down at last. I was saved from the car crash, but now I am thrust into this hell, clawing my way out just to face the cold that may very well end me instead. Death was playing a cruel game of cat and mouse with me, toying with my fate at every turn. Yet I wondered if I wanted to keep dodging death at all. Maybe this could be that time where I found her again. I wondered if I should be fighting so hard at all.

I closed my eyes and took two steps forward. I saw the night sky again. There were a couple stars out in the sky, but it was pitch black otherwise. The sky was clearing up now that the storm had passed. I turned my head to look up a steep slope. At the top of the snow-covered summit, I saw her, the old hag in all black. Her eyes were surrounded by black eye shadow and her skin was a dead man's white. She looked like a woman that had risen from a coffin mere days after death.

Again, she stared at me wordlessly. She raised her right hand and with two crooked fingers tipped with black fingernails, she pointed to her left. I closed my eyes and turned my head to the left. As my eyes closed, it seemed my eyes simultaneously opened again but this time I was back in the house and greeted by faint candlelight in an otherwise dark room.

It was strange, it was as if when I closed my eyes too tightly, I was back outside the village yet when I opened them, I was back in the house. It was just like when I was in the basement. There seemed to be a flicker of motion that I just barely caught in the corner of my eye. I turned to focus on where the motion came from, but the candles' lights did not reach that side of the room. From behind the shadows, I could hear a faint breathing.

I slowly raised my hands and curled my fingers into tight fists. Whatever lurked in that darkness, I would face it no matter what. Something deep inside of me screamed out, "Don't give up!" The house seemed like it was prepared for some strange occult ritual. There were strange red markings resembling pentagrams on the walls. On the floor, beneath my feet, there was a strange black liquid that led into the darkness.

I listened closely to the faint breathing; after a few quiet moments passed, I heard the slow slapping of four feet on the ground as the creature began to approach me out of the darkness. It was like some kind of animal preparing to pounce. It came slowly, one foot after the other, bare skin slapping against the hardwood. There was a bang at the basement door that shook the house. I felt a jolt in my heart as I looked to my left. The door was still secure, but with the second tackle, the door's wood began to crack. It was a horrid sound on such an otherwise quiet night.

I heard a blood hound's snarl from my right, and I quickly threw a fist into the general direction of the sound. My fist painfully collided with a woman's jaw. She fell to her side and again stood on all fours with her arms twisted to support her body, now arched to walk like a spider. Her neck was disgustingly contorted so that her head could be held upright in this unnatural position. The skin around her neck looked strained and white, as if the bones in her neck were going to pop out of her neck at any second.

Her head twitched from the stress of twisting to face me. The smile was completely gone from her face; her jaw was dislocated from my punch. She crawled to the left and the right like a confused cockroach, preparing to pounce. There was another collision with the basement door and the wood continued to splinter from the strain, only one hinge remained. I grabbed a long candle from the floor beside me and threw it like a spear at the demented creature crawling at me. The candle's tip went straight into its eye, a sickening mixture of wax and black blood was oozing out of its eye socket, but I couldn't care less for this mutant's pain. It began to scream like a desperate beast before death. I turned on my heel and ran toward the door.

With one last tackle, my cannibalistic host broke down the door and was barking as he slid across the kitchen floor, trying to steady himself and chase after me like a rabid dog. His wife had also straightened herself out and fixed her one good eye on me. I turned back toward the door. Sprinting toward the door, panic overtook me. "Can I make it??" I wondered. Could I open the door soon enough to escape? By the time I could check, they would be upon me. Time to think quickly. I veered to the left and raised my hands over my head.

I leapt with full force and crashed through the window. I rolled forward onto the soft snow and stopped, crouched on my feet, keeping balance with one hand. The cold snow against my hand stung with pins and needles from the rapid change in temperature. The crisp air scratched my throat as I gasped it in through my mouth, readying to run. I sprang forward and began sprinting down the road, lifting my feet, and slamming them back into the snow with every step, determined not to stumble. I ran without any regard for what was behind me, looking back would just waste my energy. Their hunt wasn't over yet, I had to keep moving. Any error could spell doom.

The road under me was a jumbled mess, as if an earthquake had hit while I was locked in the basement. My footing was un-even and I stumbled, falling face first into the snow. As I fell, I could feel my heart stop from fear. The cold stung my hot face and sent a jolt back to my heart, forcing it to beat again. It felt like jumping into a cold summer pool. I wiped the snow off my face and looked forward. Under a flickering lamp post, I saw what appeared to be a standing shadow. The figure was tall but the light didn't illuminate any of its features. The light went out and when it came back on again, I noticed that the same shadow was now facing away from me. This impossible shadow was casting itself across the floor but there was no source. It turned to the left and to my horror I saw the white face, void of life. The same face of the old woman dressed in black. It wasn't a shadow; her dress was just so dark. Another flicker of light from the lamp post, and she was gone.

Seeing her in my moment of desperation left an uneasy feeling in my stomach. Nothing made sense in this nightmarish reality. Those things in the house were not human, and this woman in all black was not human either. My head was spinning; I stood up and saw that I had tripped on a deep crack in the cement. All around me the cement was filled with cracks and behind me there were sink holes in the ground. It seemed the world around me was unraveling with my sanity. I looked at my watch, it read 1:43 am. I had been unconscious for a few hours now, but I was still sure this kind of seismic event would have woken me up, even if I was hanging.

I looked behind me, checking for my past hosts. From a little over 100 yards away, I could see their pale white faces as they crawled toward me on all fours. Their hands and feet slapped the pavement awkwardly like overgrown cockroaches. I wanted to avoid the path the woman had taken and my pursuers, so I turned to my right and ran down an alternate dark road that was just barely illuminated by the stars. I ran down the middle of the desolate, lonely road, trying not to look back.

They were still coming, they stopped just before the lamp-post the old hag was at, thankfully taking a detour before changing direction toward me. The man stopped and sniffed the air, they were hunting me relentlessly. I needed to hide. The nearest house was to my left; the house didn't have a single light on, and the driveway was empty. The bronze cross on the door seemed loose and was inverted but clearly embellished upon the door. Instead of a knocker on the door, there was a symbol of an old man on a disk with eagle wings. It reminded me of something I read about in an old religious textbook... a Faravahar? It seemed upside down as well. The house was showing signs of neglect form the outside with loose roof panels, but it was my closest option.

I reached into my pocket for my father's Swiss Army knife and jammed its blade into the keyhole. I could barely steady my breath from fear. The woman let out a high-pitched bark and again I could hear their feet slapping the pavement, coming toward me. They had caught up to me. I did not have the will to look back anymore, I forced the door open with the knife and immediately closed the door and locked it behind me.

~ IV ~

THROUGH THE VOID

The house was almost completely dark except for shards of moonlight that shined through the curtains of a nearby window and illuminated three hard wood tiles, but nothing more. I prayed for loneliness on this hellish night. I could still hear the hunters outside, running around and sniffing the air, desperately seeking their prey. Unable to see my surroundings, I could not feel safe yet even with the door between us. Paranoid thoughts raced through my head, "are the walls all up or is there a broken hole they can crawl through. Will they start smashing in the windows?"

My hands fumbled in my pockets, desperately looking for a source of light. I did not even consider searching for a light switch with those two demons searching for me. Thankfully, my tortured mind could still concoct a solution for my dire situation. I took my phone off my belt and turned on its light function. The first thing the light illuminated was a pair of pale grey eyes staring right back at me from out of a door's archway down the hall. They blinked and then were followed by white teeth. It looked like a young man, hiding behind the door, watching me with eyes that bore more fear than my own. He began to shake his head violently without a word. He seemed different from the other two, so I began to slowly walk toward him with one hand holding my phone and the other in my pocket holding my father's knife. I thought maybe he could tell me where we were and what was going on.

He did not look dangerous; he began to step back into the kitchen as I drew nearer. My phone began to flicker; its battery was low after my two days of travel. The quiet was shattered by a bark from outside. The battery died and once again I was left in darkness. My breathing became jagged from fear. I couldn't stand the torture of this night; living was such a struggle when all I wanted was a warm place to rest on this cold night. Even inside the house was still cold, only slightly better than outside.

I could hear the paint peel off the door as the monster began scratching it with their nails. A loud thump against the window made the hairs on the back of my neck stand on end. I could see the woman's pale, demented face pressed against the windowpane. Her forked tongue was licking the chilled surface, and her incessant breathing was fogging the glass. The moonlight behind her illuminated only an unoccupied square of the hardwood floor. She stared, searching to no avail, I was still shrouded in the darkness of the house against a far wall. A hand behind me pulled me into the kitchen and away from her horrid sight.

The hand on my shoulder was firm, but I felt safe. I could feel his hot breath that smelled of cigar smoke as he spoke in a hoarse whisper, "What the hell are you doing here? Is she following you too?" I could just barely make out the outlines of a face, he looked about the same age as me with a sharp jaw and a ragged beard. I couldn't make out the expression on his face, but he sounded just as scared as I felt. I wondered if he was another escapee from the house I just ran from.

"She's against the window; didn't you see her? I think her husband is hunting me too," I whispered back. He seemed to breathe a sigh of relief. "Wait, who are you talking about? What is this place?" He released my shoulder and took a step back.

"There's this old woman dressed in all black. She was following my brother and me. We were camping in the mountains on a brisk spring day around here, just a day ago. I was hiking, alone in the woods while my brother was hunting a bear. That's when I first saw her dreary figure. The black parchment hung meekly from her skeletal figure. Her long fingers were thin like the legs of spiders and her eyes awoke a primal fear in my heart. There is something retched in her gaze, something that... that just ain't right. She was staring at my brother from behind a tree while he was starting our fire. Just staring with those dead fisheyes. I approached her hesitantly and asked what she was doing. She just turned those eyes on me and opened her mouth, but no words came out. Her mouth opened wider and wider, I thought her jaw would snap off, it was inhuman. There was no sound coming out, but I felt something, I think it was helplessness. My head began to hurt, and I passed out, feeling nothing but dread, remembering her hollow eyes.

"I awoke with the same feeling of dread. It was near night-fall, but there was no fire or smoke anywhere close. I ran toward where I remembered the camp being. By the time I got there, my brother was lying dead in his tent. His face bore a look of absolute horror. I came out of the tent crying uncontrollably. I felt like there was an unearthly presence watching me. I looked around to find her, but there was nothing.

"I needed to get help, was my first thought. I took my brother's keys and found my way to our car. All its tires were slashed, and the words "Arcane Town" were written in blood on my windshield. I could feel her gaze upon me the whole time.

She was there, watching me, that sick bitch," his breath quickened, and his eyes grew livid. "I ran, panic overtook me. I found this log cabin, and here I am now. I know I'm next. She won't leave me alone. Even now, she's watching. She is always watching..." His paranoia was contagious. I remembered her under the streetlamp, she was indeed watching both of us, but his story was outrageous. I drove here through a snowstorm. It sure as hell wasn't spring only a day ago.

"It's not spring out there anymore. There was just a blizzard, and we're in a house in a small town, not a log cabin" I told him. I began to fear that my new-found host was another maniac in this town. This was a strange place, where no one and nothing could be trusted. He was no different. Slowly, some memories started to piece together. "Wait a minute. Your brother was hunting a bear in the... in the town of Pinetop- Lakeside over in Arizona?" That was where I had met the officers and the dogs with Annabel, when I realized I wanted to marry her.

"That's right... How'd you know that?" He asked in a low voice coated with suspicion.

How could I phrase it gently? "Umm, I remember going there about 5 years ago and hearing about a black bear killing a 61-year-old woman." I decided to avoid the truth. If this man really has traversed this "Arcane Town" for 5 years without knowing it, he was likely mentally unstable and dangerous. The story actually mentioned a dead 33-year-old man; I would hazard a guess that it was his brother. I needed to watch my words or else he would become the prime danger to my survival. The cold from outside was still present within the house, but I began to feel a distant warmth.

A dim light began to flicker behind an adjacent door, and I could see my host's face contort with confusion. "What the hell is that?" he asked as a door screeched to a close behind me. I felt a shiver go down my spine.

There was an instinctual fear in my heart. The same fear a bird feels when it sees a cat, the instinctual fear that cannot be denied and is so apparent that it needs no explanation. He began to stand up and walk toward the faint light behind me. "Don't go. I have a bad feeling about this. Listen, we should get out of here. Whether it's winter or spring, it doesn't matter, we need to leave this place or else she will find us," I warned. I was nervous about my new companion, but that was nothing close to the dread I felt for whatever was behind that door. Even if I could feel warmth on the other side, every fiber of my being screamed out to avoid that room no matter what.

He ignored my warning and walked past me, mesmerized by the faint light behind the door. His hand gently pushed the door open. We could feel the warmth of a fire seep into the kitchen as the door opened. There was an empty room before us, modestly furnished with a single wooden table with a rustic brown couch beside it. The fireplace housed a small flame that ate away at a few scraps of wood. My companion walked deeper into the room, and I followed behind him, hoping to see what my heart dreaded so fiercely.

Before the fire there was a huddled mass, completely hidden under a blanket that bore the same strange marking that I noticed on the door. The huddled mass was unlike anything I had ever witnessed. Its presence felt like an abomination. I could not fathom what was under that shabby blanket, man, or beast, but I could feel that it was unnatural. I placed a firm hand on my companion's shoulder to hold him back. "We don't know what's under there. This is a strange place; we need to get out of here now," I insisted. He pulled his shoulder out of my grasp. I could see him better in the light. He was in his thirties but had some streaks of grey in his unkempt hair and beard. His eyes were wide and grey, fixated on the bundle.

The mass under the blanket shivered, it looked like it was no larger than an infant. My companion did not heed my warnings, he continued to inch toward it. It could be a pale white child, with hollow eyes, and blood lining those empty eyes. It could be a child that would haunt me forever, watching every step I took, like an omnipotent God. Perhaps, this was the old hag's child. Or maybe it would be an empty blanket. Under that blanket could be any kind of horror, but my companion's curiosity was insatiable and as was mine, so I stayed to witness. Some things are better left alone, but fate does not care, it drives us wherever it pleases. Even when we know better, it will steer us toward where we are meant to be.

His hand slowly drew back the blanket. It revealed something, but I could not understand it. Its form was that of an apparition in opposed to a beast. The mass was like a gas, indistinct but it had a general form. It had the form of a small child, but there were no eyes, no features, simply a vague form. More akin to the shadow of a child caused from a flickering candle than the actual child. A form so vague, that I am still not sure whether I imagined that it had a form at all. If it was related to the old woman, I shudder to think what she truly is.

He jumped back appalled by this abomination that he had uncovered. The ground began to shake, and the fire began to flicker. The abomination began to give a deafening whistle that made my head spin and ache. I felt confused, terrified, and depressed all at once. I could feel blood dripping down from my nose. I fell to my knees and struggled to look up. The abomination changed its form and began to slither toward my companion like a snake across the dingey beige rug, it looked like a living black ooze. He tried to drag himself away from the abomination and toward me through the disorientating screams of the abomination. Discombobulated, I tried to drag myself toward the backdoor to escape this hell. My head throbbed and my nose kept bleeding as my hands desperately reached for the door. To my relief it began to turn. As I looked back, I saw my companion reach out an aged hand lined with creases and moles. His hair was turning white, and his face became gaunt during the seconds of watching him. I watched as the abomination entered the pores of his body and sucked out his youth from the inside. He began to choke as thick blood flowed from his nose into his mouth. His lips were wordlessly begging, "Please... please," but I pulled myself through the threshold and shut the door, locking that abomination away once more.

There was nothing left to be done. Playing hero would have led to my death as well. There was no other choice. The abomination was not something to be trifled with and every instinct in my body repelled me from that thing.

I was alone once again, but I was still alive. Maybe I should have submitted to it. After all, what was I doing in this town anyway? What was I running for, fighting for? My doubts consumed my mind as I stood up and started to walk forward through the thick snow in the empty backyard. I opened the metal gate with a creak and found myself on a new street.

Not a soul was present, human, or otherwise. All I could hear was the gentle sound of snow falling. In that short time that felt like an eternity, the snow had started up again. I took a deep breath of the crisp air and closed my eyes. For a moment, I was home, walking toward an open door. I could hear a singular scream; my heart began to pound against my chest as I dashed to the door.

Losing my breath, I quickly opened my eyes and inspected my surroundings. There was nothing but snow-covered cars, trees, and houses. The street was a uniform black. Some streetlamps were cracked, and others were simply off. A chill overcame me, and I shivered, again there was a bitter taste in my mouth. I reached into my pocket for some gum, but both of my pockets were empty save for my pocketknife. I let out a lonely sigh. Walking forward, I noticed a light from within a parked car. This car looked like the snow had recently been dusted off it, but a few scattered dustings of snow kept a thin layer on the pickup truck. It was a small, dingy, and blue little thing that was covered with patches of rust.

I walked up to the driver's side where the light was strongest. As I drew closer, I heard the unpleasant scratching noise of a radio without signal. A reminder of how isolated and truly alone I was. I tapped on the glass, but there was no response. I cuffed some of my coat's sleeve around my hands and wiped off a patch of frost from the window. Through the fog of the window, I saw a man bent over with his head against the top of the steering wheel. There was no blood dripping from the steering wheel, but it was stained red.

I immediately opened the door; this man may have suffered from a concussion or worse. I gently grabbed onto his damp forehead and pulled him off the steering wheel. My skin crawled as I heard a slurping sound. There was a cardboard thick layer of skin and flesh clinging to the wheel. His skin was stuck to the steering wheel; he suffered a scalp avulsion when I began to pull. His face was blue; he had been out here for a long time, dead. As I stared at him, my head began to spin. My breathing was quickly accelerating, my heart was pounding until I felt myself becoming lightheaded.

I began to shake compulsively. Hand raised to the neck. Check for a pulse. Constant scratching in my head. Cold searing my skin. No pulse. Damned radio still scratching. Blood on my hands. Memories flooding in. Not him, but her. She was lying there. I was too late. It was over. Limp hands. No pulse. We were out of time. So much left unsaid. So many years, gone. No more laughter. No more joy. No silver lining. No more time. Hands covered in blood. Face covered in tears. Gasping for air. Reaching for reality. Lost in darkness, alone.

I fell over into the snow, wiping my bloody hands in the snow, hyperventilating. The pure white became an impure and nasty dark red. My chest began to sting with pain as I gasped for air, wailing in the silent, lonely night. I screamed with pain as the memories broke down my mind's walls. The hot sears dug into my ribs and I howled like a mad man at the moon, insanity was clawing at my mind with racing thoughts. All the world was fading to darkness; I stood up and ran toward the only light I could see. There was no other lit path to be taken unless I wanted to go back to the mad house I had just come from. Once I was under the lamp's light my eyes blurred. Eyes so used to the darkness. I shielded my eyes from the bright until the light flickered off.

I stared in awe at what I saw in the darkness to my left, in all this hell stood a vision of heaven. There she stood dressed in all white, my one and only, my purpose, my passion, my fire, my life. She gave me a faint smile and slowly began to flicker away as the lights above me began to flicker back on. Her form was that of an apparition, scarcely there, but real enough to be perceived without any doubt.

"NO! God, Damn it! No! Annabel, come back to me!" I screamed, I dug my nails into my skin, feeling my blood under my nails. It all felt real, it all felt painfully real. Mania overtook me. I ran after her fading image, into the darkness. There was no fear in my heart; nothing was inside of me but a desperate need to be with her one more time. Without her, all the world is simply an illusion, she was my truth, my anchor. She was passing through a wall into a dark house, her gentle hand outstretched toward me. I reached out to feel her warmth again. The hand vanished behind the wall, far out of my reach.

In my mind, there was no thought, only an all-consuming need to be with her. I let out a roar as I shut my eyes tight and raised my hands over my head, leaping at the wall with every ounce of strength my body could muster.

If I could just reach her, hold her one more time, everything could be set right. The past could be rewritten. I could be happy. Everything would make sense again. The blood would be washed from my hands.

I burst through the door. The scream came from the kitchen. Within an instant I was there and stood aghast at the sight of Annabel lying against the counter with her hand and blonde hair soaked in her own blood. She was clinging to a hole on the left side of her chest. Her bright red blood flowed like a forceful river across her chest and onto the floor. My eyes darted to the right to see a masked man holding a gun.

Rage overtook me. I ran at him. Bullets flew past me, but I knew no fear. When my hands met his face, I knew no mercy. I grabbed his face and hammered it against the cupboard until the back of his head was dripping blood. I held his face before me, his eyes were rolling in his skull and with a feeling of pure hatred my right fist crossed the left side of his face. The right side of his face bounced off the corner of my dinner table. I grabbed his gun out of his limp hand and held the gun to his head. He did not flinch. He might have been dead or unconscious, I couldn't tell which.

Every fiber of my being wanted to pull the trigger and make sure he was dead, but revenge would not save my sweet Annabel. I first clicked the small button on the side of the handgun and took out the main clip of ammo, next I emptied the chamber. I ripped out my phone from my pocket and called the ambulance as I rushed to my love's side.

"It's all going dark... Please, hold me," she whispered. There was barely any life left in her. Her eyes stared past me at someone else, someone I could not perceive. It looked like she tried to whisper "no," to that invisible person.

I took a washcloth from the countertop and pushed it against the wound to slow the bleeding. Tears were running down my face. I knew death was just around the corner for her no matter how hard I tried. She was already turning pale. "I'm here now. I'm sorry, I'm so sorry I was too late. God damn it. I love you. I love you so much; it's going to be alright." I lied; I didn't want her to be afraid. In my mind, I began to beg and plead with God to save her. I bartered my soul for her. He is known to hand out miracles, why couldn't he spare one miracle for me? Let her live, let our love continue, let us bare children. Just please don't take away all I care about in this empty world.

She raised her hand and gently put it onto my cheek, I held it there with my hand. "It's alright. We'll see each other on the other side in due time. I love you James. Neither life nor death can change that. It's alright, I'm not afraid... But please, live James." I felt the life in her hand fade, and then silence. She died with a smile on her face with her green eyes fixed on me, now dilated.

I passed through the wall with no resistance. I appeared in a cozy room with a table and a couple relaxing couches surrounding it. They were suede couches just like the ones in our home. I scanned the room and immediately found her, dressed in a beautiful, long white dress with thin straps. She wore a gentle smile and looked at me with that special look in her eyes reserved solely for me. I stared at her as if it were the first time I had ever seen her.

She took regal steps toward me, her dress swishing gently around her long, smooth legs. "What are you doing here James?" She had a playful look on her face, speaking as if she was scolding a naughty child. She raised her left eyebrow with an inquisitive look.

"Is... Is it really you?" I asked. I couldn't believe that my wish had come to fruition. I felt life pour into my body. It was as if the entire day was washed off me by a cool rain. Being with her again took away all my pain and sorrow and replaced it with triumph. "I finally found you, just like I promised."

She looked at me with penetrating eyes as if she was searching for some hidden truth in my face. "Do you know where you are?" she asked, this time with a grave voice. The smile completely vanished from her face and was replaced by a very somber look that left me unsettled. "You shouldn't be *here*; you should never be *here* my love."

"I don't care where I am Annabel! I am with you; therefore, I am happy!" I replied, unafraid of whatever cruel truths awaited me. If I was with her, I was home. She smiled, and I saw a warm glow in her green eyes, still beautiful in the dark room. Our room was lit only by the moon's silver light. I smiled; it was automatic. It's all I can ever do when I see her smile.

Tears began to form in her eyes. I came to her and wrapped my hands around her gentle shoulders and drew her closer into my embrace, onto the couch. I held her tightly and breathed in the sweet smell of lilacs once more. My eyes began to fill with tears of joy. It was divine to be able to hold her once more. I thought the day would never come again. I thought I was damned to walk the Earth alone and miserable, awaiting death forever.

"James, I am so happy to see you again, to be held by you again, but this isn't right. You can't be *here*." I couldn't understand why she was so insistent upon me leaving. "This is not heaven, hell, nor earth. This is an in between. It's a void where monsters hunt each other until the end of days; it's not meant for humans. Those creatures want to consume you. You see yourself as a body here, but all you are is a wandering spirit, vulnerable to them. You are lost, you have to find your way and escape from *here*. Please, stop wandering and keep living. It was my last request after all. I know you remember," she was pleading with me. Her bright eyes stared at me; her narrow eyebrows were contorted with sincere concern.

"No, I won't leave this place. Not without you. I do not fear any beast or monster, I will face them all for you," I was not about to lose her again. Not after all I had been through to find her. "All the world can burn and wait because all I want is to be beside you. Nothing else matters."

I looked toward the dark window, leading out to the cold that I had just escaped. I wondered what it would be like to explore this frozen wasteland for all eternity while holding onto the singular hope of seeing Annabel from time to time. I saw my reflection in the glass and beyond that there looked like there was an old decrepit woman dressed in all black with pasty white skin watching us. Was she in the room with us or just staring in from the other side? Annabel noticed my distraction, so she gently touched my chin with her fingers and brought my face toward hers.

"James, I only came here to help you leave this place. I don't belong here either. I wanted to save you from going down the wrong path. No matter what you do, I can't come back to life. The past cannot be changed and it's not your fault either, but you must live on. You chose to chase after death, now she is following you closely, but it is not your place to chase after death. Death always follows and stalks life, it's the duty of the living to chase after life! You need to live the life ordained to you no matter how hard it feels. She does not want to take you, but if you do not stop tempting fate, she will keep you, trapped here, alone, forever. I will only be able to visit you when your soul has been beaten and battered and is ready to fade into nothing. Stop this chase; stop running from your pain. The love I remember wasn't a runner."

Her words burned deep into my heart. I was finally happy, I had finally found her, but all for naught. "I don't want to live without you. If I go back, I will be alone out there too. Here, at least I can hope to see you again once more."

"Don't let the pain devour your soul. I loved a greater man than that. The man I loved knew that we carried each other within ourselves. He knew that he was never truly alone no matter where he was. That was how powerfully we loved. We will have an eternity together, but only if you live your life to the fullest and carry my memories, my soul with you. You can't give up on life. You never gave up before, don't start now."

"An eternity?" I asked, the words made a painful lump in my throat.

"Yes, if you live the life you are given. There is more left for you to do for the people of the world. Everything comes in its proper time." When the reaper had said that I was alone, I knew Annabel was with me then. She was and is within me, but yet I am without her. It pained me, but I knew she was right. It was not the natural order for a man to chase death. I needed to leave this place. My desperation, my pain, my fear, and my loneliness made my soul vulnerable in this place filled with strange beasts that prey upon the lost.

We faced each other, still hand in hand. "How can I survive all of this?" I asked. I smiled as I watched her beautiful face twist into a spectacular smile once more. The room felt brighter as I stared at those soft, pink lips that had so many times before kissed away all my pain. She was elated, knowing she could save her love's soul instead of being the cause of its damnation. Even in death, she was protecting me.

"There is a forest that will lead you out of this void. The forest will engulf you if you give into your despair. Hold tightly to your resolve to survive or else you will never reach freedom. Make sure you stay on the path, do not stray from it for a second or else the nightmares of this unholy land will be upon you. An Ankou, one of Death's guides, will be waiting for you at the end of the trail. You chose to pursue death, but now I beg of you; pursue life, pursue life for you and all of those that need you to-morrow... and for me. You can make it my love. I believe in you now and forever," she replied.

I looked at her one last time. Her gorgeous figure was so gentle and warm. Her bright green eyes shined with an unparalleled sense of life. It was as if her eyes could see through the impurities of the world and straight to the truth. Her lips were moist and full like fresh rose pedals covered with morning dew. I was overtaken by passion as I drew her towards me to kiss her one last time. Her breath entered my body and healed the wounds in my heart. Her eyes slowly closed as my lips conveyed my deep and undying love. Within that moment, with our eyes closed, I could see a grove with an old oak tree and a house nearby. In the house, we sat at the dining table enjoying break-fast, pancakes and eggs, with our daughter. The refrigerator had beautiful drawings that were signed by our daughter, Marie. A house, a tree, and a happy family. Another instant and I could see an old, wrinkled couple sitting under that same oak tree. Its leaves were a vibrant red and there were small children running in the distance, leaping into heaps of leaves. A young couple was bringing us tea as we sat watching our family at play. A lifetime of happiness played out before my eyes. It was hope for a better life, someday when peace would finally come and take this vagabond to eternity.

"I will always love you," I told her, breathless, as I drew my face away from hers. For a moment, she was breathless too. A heavy door appeared behind us. She hid her face with her hand as she grew red.

"I love you too. I will be waiting for you as long as it takes," she replied with tears. I willed myself away from her and toward the door. Once the knob began to turn, my whole world disappeared, and I suddenly found myself in a pitch-black forest with trees in every direction, creating a canopy of darkness. The stars up above and the red moon ahead of me were scarcely visible through the interweaving branches of the trees. The starlight illuminated the green of the leaves overhead. The light almost felt like a familiar friend. Just as my head turned to follow the light to its source, a cold wind blew across my face, making me wince as the clouds covered the light momentarily.

I was alone again, but not as entirely as before. I had my eternal companion locked within my heart. I could almost feel her gentle hand upon my cheek, reassuring me that I could survive this trial. I took a singular step forward. Once my foot touched the forest's overgrown floor, a dirt path appeared and led me forward through the thick forest. With every step, it seemed like the stars grew brighter and the clouds were torn asunder to reveal their luminous light.

I followed the path to life vigilantly. There were rustling sounds in the bushes and in the tops of trees as I continued my journey. I ignored the eyes staring at me between the trees.

Those hungry eyes, waiting for me to falter so they may feast upon my vulnerable soul. I could make out the shapes of wolves and contorted demons against the dark foliage. Some seemed to tower up to 10 feet in height from the dark outlines. The eyes began to wear down on my nerves. When I began to grow weary, the darkness began to engulf me until my eyes could barely see the path before me and the stars became dim specks of white. I no longer knew where the path continued. I tried to keep walking in the same direction as before, but even that was a guess following the initial shock of losing the path.

From behind me, came the shrill screams of a man in agony. I could hear the enraged barks of a dog reverberate throughout the forest from far away as beasts tore the clothes and flesh from their victim. I wondered if they would devour me in the same horrid way. The panic overtook me and I began to run forward frantically. This was no longer the village. There was nowhere to hide, just trees that were surrounded by ominous eyes. The whole forest became filled with screams of men and women. It was as if all who were to be punished were thrown into this one forest to be tortured by the indigenous fiends. The victims and their punishers.

A root or a hand, I could not tell which, grabbed my leg as I ran. I fell to my knees; breathing heavily as invisible hands wrung my neck and clawed at my back. Their breath rattled as they dug their nails into me. Laughter began to ring in my ears as the nails dug deeper and deeper into my back. The screaming in the distance was tuned out by the menacing laughter in my ears.

The pain was indescribable and came from all sides; I was surrounded by these vultures. No pain or illness could compare to the feeling of their inhuman claws. It was more than the pain of their claws; it was a pain that felt like it dug deep and scratched my bones. My entire being screamed out in pain as my skin broke against their onslaught. I gasped for air as the wolves howled, digging relentlessly. Their claws searched for my heart, hoping its warmth could give their soulless vessels the feeling of life.

I tried to fight back against my assailants, but my strength was like that of a child when compared to these beasts. For a moment, I wondered if it wouldn't be better to just die there. No more struggling, just surrender.

"James, don't give up," she whispered in my ear. I heard her whisper against all the laughter and my screams.

Then the world went silent. I opened my eyes, and I was sitting under a great oak tree, crying. I felt so painfully alone and lost. The sun was setting on the day and the lower it went, the greater became my feeling of dread. "Hey there handsome, what're you crying for? You look like a little lost bunny. Did you scurry away too far from home looking for something?" asked a sweet and familiar voice.

I felt found again before I even looked up. Annabel was coming toward me in a blue summer dress with red roses printed on it. It was strange though, she looked so young, like she was 18 again... And I was the one under our tree. "Annabel... am I... am I dead? Is this real?" I asked, stuttering between gasps as I wiped away my tears.

She sighed and stood in front of me with her hands on her hips. "How many times do we have to have this talk James? You're not some frightened child."

The tears began to flow down my face anew. "But I'm so alone without you... There's nothing to go back to. Why should I want to keep going?"

Her soft features broke with sympathy as she looked down at me. Her forehead wrinkled with concern and eyes narrowed as they absorbed every detail of my pain. She wiped my tears with one hand and held my hand with the other.

"My dearest James. Words cannot describe how much I love you. I will always be with you in our memories. It feels like you have no purpose because you haven't found it yet. And I promise you, you will find purpose once more, very soon. There will be people that need your help. For now, I know it will be tough. I know it will seem pointless my love, but please; for me, for you, for anything you can hold onto, LIVE." She lifted me up and my world went black.

I opened my eyes, but it was still dark and smelled like wet grass. I rolled over and saw stars in a night sky, outlined by the edges of trees. When I raised my head and looked around me, I saw the motionless bodies of the beasts that had attacked me scattered all about. There were no stab wounds on any of them. It seemed like some silent guardian had flung them off me like pestering gnats.

More beasts stood by the edge of the woods with hateful glares, but now they were too nervous to approach me. The clouds cleared away and the stars began to show their radiance as well. The beasts ran back into the brush as the radiance lit the night and brought beauty upon an otherwise macabre forest. The trees no longer harbored unknown terrors. I could perceive every branch and the emptiness around each trunk in the new light. There was no longer anything left to fear. The white light from the skies radiated to the rest of my body and the flesh across my back, mending the wounds as if by magic.

I came to a fork in my path. There was a smooth dirt path to my left that led back to the well-lit village, and there was a dirt path to my right with outlying roots that led further into the darkness of the forest, only illuminated by the red moon up above.

Did I feel hopeful for my future? No, there was little hope, but I chose to carry on. I chose the right path. Whatever lady fate chooses for me is what I must live with. It is not my place to choose when I have had enough. That is not the man Annabel fell in love with. She fell in love with a soldier who never gave up, no matter what.

For her I will carry on. With her memory in my heart, I will survive, and someday... Someday, maybe, I will be happy again. The eyes that glared at me from behind the trees looked desperate as my journey began to wind down to its end. They could feel my resolve hardening. Soon there would be nothing for them to feed upon, and they would have to go back to hunting one another in an eternal struggle.

They growled and snarled at me from the borders of the darkness and light as I walked upon my path. I could feel their hatred; they wanted nothing other than to tear me apart, but I would not falter upon my path. A bush ahead of me rustled and my old demon host from earlier burst out like a police hound on a chase. She was still running on all fours with her neck twisted unnaturally. I reached into my coat pocket and felt my father's old pocket knife. I dodged to the right as the demon rounded upon me once more. Her obscene smile was still on her face with one eye hanging out of the socket and the other bulging out toward me. It began to lick its lips with a forked tongue. I readied my knife as it pounced again. I caught it and stabbed my knife into its back. It began thrashing with its legs and hands, but I held it tightly with my left arm as I kept stabbing with my right.

The desperate beast bore its fangs into my left shoulder. I stabbed the knife into the back of its skull with all my force. I covered my bleeding shoulder with my hand and quickly peered into the surrounding forest. The eyes were growing nearer. The sight of blood made the beasts overcome their fear of the light. I concentrated on my memories of Annabel to act as my shield. I looked down the path toward the direction I had to go and began running, clutching my shoulder.

Behind me, I heard wild dogs rampaging through the foliage after me. Demons scurrying on all fours, greedily slapping the mutts out of their way as they all desperately chased after the only satisfying meal in the forest. There was one wolf that broke out from the rest of the pack and I could hear its panting and snarls as if the sound came from just beside me. Drawing my father's knife, I quickly stepped back and thrust the razor's edge into the wolf's skull. The knife pierced its skull just behind its eye. I quivered as I felt its skull break and give way to the blade. The knife was lodged in the skull, but I pulled with all my might until it was free. It was a memento from my father, not something to be left in a corpse in the middle of some unknown world. I was close to the end of the long path now and the two corpses kept the other fiends at bay.

The path finally ended; I had reached a clearing. The old woman in black was waiting for me as promised. As soon as she was within my gaze, all the other beasts became meek and stopped their pursuit. They retreated into the forest like scolded children.

She stared at me with all knowing eyes and for the first time I saw a crooked smile on her deeply aged face. The reaper stood with her back to a tall tree with deep roots. Drawing near, I saw that her eyes were deep in her skull and she wore no eye shadow at all. Perhaps I was simply confused, but her eyes looked green now that I stood close to her, a dead green. She was an archaic woman who observed silently, except for now.

She slowly opened her mouth and spoke in a croaky voice. It sounded like she had not spoken for years, as if speaking was new to her. "Have you learned? Do you understand now?" she asked with slow words. Her complexion still sent shivers down my spine, but I knew not to fear her.

"Yes, it pains me, but I understand. I choose to pursue life. All things come in due time, but it is not my time," I answered. There was a warm hand on my face. Its warmth took away all the cold of the night. It was Annabel's hand; I knew her touch. She wasn't there in physical form, but her ethereal presence would be with me forever. I whispered to her in the night so the reaper would not hear my words. "It hurts like a knife in my heart to admit that you are gone, but I'll carry you with me forever until the time comes that I find you again."

"Love is difficult, child. It leaves a hole when it is torn away, but I knew you would find your way out of this dark place. There is something special about your spirit. I wish you the best of luck James Aman," she said with a crooked smile. In her knowing eyes, I could see a look of expectation with just a tinge of affection. She expected something from me, but before I could ask what it was, she began to fade away into the moon's red glow.

My eyes blurred and when I opened them next, I awoke before the bridge to the village. I looked above me and saw the cliff where I first saw the woman in black. I was no longer cold; I was no longer afraid. I strode into the village with a heavy heart.

~ V ~

MR. GRIM

I just finished telling my story. I turned to the waitress and ordered a cheeseburger with fries, I was famished. It was my first meal in what felt like days. She looked like a college student, a cute one. Dark red hair and deep blue eyes that exuded a feeling of calm. I sat across from a strange companion, a well-groomed man in a black suit, wearing a black tie against a white button up shirt, and black shoes. He seemed intrigued by my story. "So you saw the other side? It seems that you lost either way faced with those choices," he said in a somber voice.

My companion was out of place in this small town; he obviously did not belong with these rural folk. He wore a large black diamond ring on his right hand that matched his onyx black cuff links. I found him strange from the moment I walked into the diner. I woke up at the base of the hill before the bridge and walked into the village. This time, the village was much brighter with all of the lights on and well-kept buildings. The villagers had pride in their home. Despite the blizzard, the gas station was open, and a kind resident offered me a ride to the village diner when he heard how hungry I was. The villager was dressed in plaid with jeans.

The man dropped me off in front of the diner with words of, "God bless and stay safe out there!"

I entered the diner and was greeted by an equally warm atmosphere. The place was busy and a hostess hurried to greet me. Out of the corner of my eye I saw a man dressed in a smart black suite. The gentleman looked like he had been waiting for someone at this diner. When I appeared, he immediately came to my side and spoke with me cordially. He acted as if he had known me for many years. He butted in and requested a table for two from the hostess.

His mannerisms were also strange. He had no interest in inspecting his surroundings; it was as if he had been to this diner a hundred times before, but no one recognized him. He was a stranger in what seemed a familiar land.

After ordering nothing but a slice of apple pie and black coffee, he handed the menu back to the waitress carefully. This was the one thing that he raised his gaze for. He eyed her hand closely, making sure their hands did not touch. As soon as the menu left his hands, he began to wipe his hands with a napkin. The man seemed like a textbook germaphobe.

"Yeah, no matter what choice I made, I suppose it was a loss. I figure, at least I did right by Annabel's wishes. That must be the lesser of two evils, right?" I laughed. It was a bitter laugh. "I had almost lost myself. I could have been wandering in the darkness forever, searching for her, but she saved me. She showed me the silver lining that I could not see. Even in death, she was with me. She's right here with me now even." I pointed to my heart.

"Ah, my apologies James, but it is not my place to judge. Yes, souls that have once been bound by love are never truly apart. The soul is an amazing thing. You carry a trace of her within you. I feel like I can see her in your eyes. In some ways, it is as if she never died," he said. He raised his eyes from his folded hands and looked me straight in the eyes with a scrutinizing gaze. "But we both know that she is in fact dead, and she is not coming back. Her presence with you is something entirely different. I am sure it hurts, but to pursue her and the dream of being with her is not just futile but dangerous for it is the same as pursuing death. Death pursues you and all that ever lived from the day of your births. There is no need to pursue Death, it will find you in due time, but you need to pursue life on your own. Life is fleeting; it is forever running away from you. Take pleasure in the simple things. Speaking of which, here is my pie." He cut his warm slice of apple pie with surgical precision and took a bite. He closed his eyes as he savored the treat. "You need to try some of this pie, James. They bake it fresh every day!" he smiled as he took another bite.

The truth slowly began to sink in. Even after all my pain, she was still dead, and nothing could ever change that. Her spirit would always live on within me, but it didn't change the fact that I could never hold her again or speak to her again. The only way I could do that is in death, but I was already down that path and it was not the right direction.

He placed a slice from his pie onto my plate and looked at me with restlessness as if asking what was keeping me down. I begrudgingly ate the pie, and to my delight it was amazing. It was a slice of sheer joy. It was just the right amount of tart and sweet and made with fresh apples. "I apologize for your loss. It is the pain of this world. You can't save everyone. By living we all become victims of injustice and likely make others victim to our own actions too, but so is the cycle of this world. Justice is not of this world but the next." He was so grim, but there was some degree of truth in what he said.

"That's a tough pill to swallow," I replied. Still sucking the taste of the pie from my teeth.

My companion chuckled gently at me from across the table. "Surely though, you are resilient enough to keep moving forward. Do not disappoint me, James. I have high hopes for your future. Just make sure to show me your number one trait; the one thing that makes you, you." He gave a forced smile. It looked odd on his stern, middle aged face.

I gave a fake smile back. All my happiness was a mask. It was all for show. Inside, I foolishly held onto the hope of seeing visions of my wife in my dreams. Someday, when the time comes, I will see her again. I hope when that day comes, I may tell her about how wonderful my life became. I will tell her about the people I helped, the lives I changed, the adventures I embarked upon, but today... Today I only have what's left of her in memories of a different time that had passed and will never again be, but tomorrow will be different. Time can heal all wounds and alas, life is only transient. This man was right, death is eternal and so is the thereafter, but life comes only once. It is my duty to Annabel and myself to live it right and to its most.

I tried to remember what it was that made me unique, why Annabel ever loved a man like me. As I recalled our many years together, it dawned on me. I persevere with a smile. It's what Annabel admired about me most, and it's what the reaper and this man valued in me too. A genuine smile started to spread across my face. I knew that I could face tomorrow. I had to choose to chase after life and hold onto the hope that this life that was still gifted to me bore a meaning, a purpose.

He finished his pie with a faint grin and touched the napkin to the corners of his mouth with utmost care. Every move was incredibly calculated by this strange, but amiable man of the world. "I have a parting gift for you James. The river of time heals all things. I suspect you may find some use for this in your future." He handed me a silver pocket watch with a train on the front and a rose with thorns on the back. It was a beautiful gift, it looked handcrafted.

"Thank you for listening... Hmph, well I don't even know your name, but you helped me through the hardest juncture in my life. What's your name?" I asked. He never asked my name, but somehow, he had known it from the moment we met.

The man sitting opposite of me stood up and gently pushed in his chair. "You may call me Mr. Grim. It has been a pleasure, but I must see to a few business matters now. Take care of yourself James. Hopefully, I will see more of you soon." He gave me an eerie wink and turned to leave after leaving a handful of dollars on the table.

I stared after him as he exited the small, poorly lit diner. He was very careful not to touch anyone on his way out except for a larger elderly man eating an order of ribs near the front counter. Mr. Grim placed one hand on the man's shoulder and whispered something in his ear.

I stayed an hour longer, simply enjoying the warmth of the diner and taking advantage of the free refills of the coffee. Mr. Grim had left enough money on the table for both of us and a generous tip. "Would you like another refill, sir?" asked the waitress cordially. Her nametag read Sarah Briston.

"Yes please, Ms. Briston," I replied, holding out my mug for another cup of coffee. It was nice to have some caffeine without poison for once. I laughed at the thought, "Another simple pleasure I suppose."

I sat drinking my coffee and contemplating my night. The reaper woman, the monsters, Annabel, and this strange Mr. Grim all made this the eeriest and longest night of my life. It was time for some rest. Whatever tomorrow brings, I'll face it.

Annabel is within me for eternity, but I am without her within this transient life. I held onto the warmth of her memory, a fragment of her soft spirit, and I hoped that I may see her again someday when this transient life passes. Tomorrow, I will pursue life once more so that I may greet her with a smile and a story of a meaningful journey when I reach the end of my path. When that time comes, I will know exactly where to find her, under a tree with deep roots.

I turned the pocket watch over in my hand a few times, it was flawless. I pressed the button on the top to check the time. I gasped as I looked inside. The time was right, but the image on the neighboring side was absurd. Mr. Grim must have walked in with this watch, but somehow it had this image waiting for whomever he gave it to. He must have known that I would come. Tears welled up in my eyes at the image of Annabel, in a small circle just opposite of the time. She was smiling back at me in the picture, just as radiant as I remembered. In the reflection of the glass, I could see my eyes too, no longer hazel but green just like hers.

END

~ VI ~

EPILOGUE

"Please tell me everything that happened," requested the investigator with a soft voice. His name was James. He had dull green eyes, his worn-out jeans and shabby brown coat were off-putting but the empathetic look in his eyes made you feel comfortable. He gently patted my back, trying to sooth my nerves. "I can't help you unless I know more." His kind countenance turned stern.

I sipped the glass of water he had passed me. I felt my heartbeat slow, and the cotton balls in my throat clear away.

"We... just came back from visiting his mother in Fayetteville, North Carolina. It was a six-and-a-half-hour trip back. By the time we were back in West Virginia, it was growing dark. He was driving us through the twilight as I stared out the window, admiring the beautiful greenery.

"Soon, it was completely dark, but we were almost home. Out of the corner of my eye, I saw a dark figure in the woods; he was walking in the same direction we were driving. When I turned my head back to look at him, I saw no one there.... It was just the darkness of the woods and the green of the leaves. I asked my husband if he saw anything; he shook his head."

Tears started to well up in my eyes again. James had an understanding look on his face. I tried my best and kept going.

"We reached our quiet home overlooking a field. When I looked up at our home, I didn't feel the relief I thought I would after a 6-and-a-half-hour trip. Instead, I felt apprehensive. My husband... Nathan... Nathan could tell I wasn't comfortable.

"He wrapped me in his arms and rocked me gently. 'Welcome home my sweet Lily, we made it back in one piece. Let's get some sleep.' I took his hand as we both grabbed a suitcase from the trunk and dragged it up to the front door.

"I looked inside our window and saw a huddled mass on the floor in the corner of my eye. 'Oh my God, look Nathan, look!' I screamed.

"He looked, and this time he saw something too, but he wouldn't admit it, yet. 'Jesus Lily, you've gotta calm down! No one's been to our house while we've been gone. It's too long a road to just walk, and I don't see a car.' He tried to reassure me, but I knew him well enough to see the fear in his eyes.

"As he turned the key, I saw his other hand reach for his hip. He slowly opened the door, anticipating an estranged home-less man. We peered into the darkness and saw nothing; both glancing into the corner where we thought we saw a balled-up figure. Nathan flicked on the lights and we both breathed a sigh of relief. Our home was exactly as we had left it.

"The air in the house felt thick, as if a heavy rain were coming. 'I'm exhausted!' I exclaimed as we huddled on the couch and closed a half open window.

"We were on the couch, enjoying each other's warmth. He was gently stroking my hair and I was resting my head on his chest, falling into an easy sleep. He kissed my hazel hair as we both fell asleep.

"I opened my eyes some hours later to a tapping sound coming from outside. It sounded like the wind was pushing a branch onto our window. 'What an annoying tree,' I yawned.

"He snorted as he woke up. 'Hmmm? A tree, what tree? There's no tree that close to our house,' he replied. My heart skipped a beat and I could feel his heart throbbing under my head. Nathan slowly got up and took out his gun from his holster lying on the ground. 'Get lost or else I'll shoot, got it!?' he was screaming at the window.

"The tapping wouldn't stop, so he started to inch toward the window with the curtains drawn. I hid behind the coffee table. The tapping was getting louder and louder, turning into banging that shook the window frame as Nathan grew closer. Something unsettling was waiting on the other side of that curtain. It sounded like the window could shatter at any moment. Just as Nathan's hand reached for the curtains, the sporadic banging stopped. He pulled back the curtains. There was nothing out there but the darkness of night, save for a few stars, glimmering at an insurmountable distance.

"'Do you think it's gone?' I asked.

"Nathan spoke without turning his head from the window, 'I really don't know. There's still no car in the driveway. No way some asshole just walked up here.'

"We listened, but we heard nothing but crickets for about twenty minutes. Nathan closed the curtain and turned away from the window satisfied. 'Case closed; it was just some God damned squirrel. What? You still look worried,' he said.

"I tried to feign a smile, but I couldn't. 'I don't know Nathan. I'm not satisfied with it just being a squirrel at this time of night. Hell, I don't think a possum could bang on the window the way whatever that had been did!' I exclaimed.

"'Well, what do you want me to do?' he shouted.

"I kissed him on the lips to calm him down. We wrapped our arms around each other and once again we felt alright. 'You always bring me back down to earth,' he told me. 'I'm sorry I was yelling.' I had never seen him this unnerved before.

"'I love you. Let's go to bed,' I told him. My gentle tugs on his arm guided him drowsily up the steps until we found ourselves safely in bed."

Back in the diner, James was busily scratching notes into his legal pad, brushing away his shoulder length mahogany hair with every few ticks. Noticing my pause, he looked up at me, furrowing his eyebrows. "I take it you two didn't sleep well for very long?" he asked.

"You're right, James, it wasn't a squirrel knocking on the window. Nathan woke up to the sound of banging against the downstairs window, again. He woke up cursing and reaching for his handgun, a reliable Glock 19. 'I'm coming too,' I said, hurriedly putting on my slippers. I could not lie alone in our room while he went downstairs to check on the dark unknown.

"He grumbled some kind of dissention, but I came with him regardless. I didn't want to be helpless; just waiting for the effects of whatever would transpire downstairs. Both of his hands were on his Glock, pointing straight toward wherever he was looking like a police officer. The rhythmic banging came to an abrupt halt and was replaced by a singular boom, mixed with the sound of shattering glass. No footsteps, no breathing, only shattering glass.

"I could see perspiration accumulate on the back of his neck in the dark. Neither of us uttered a word as we descended those stairs into the darkness. All sound had stopped save for my breath and Nathan's. The wind had stopped, the birds had flown away, the crickets were dead or gone, and the house was still.

"My feet cringed within my rubber slippers at the site of the shattered glass shimmering like morning dew in the moonlight, but they were not crushed into dust from any footsteps. No one had come in. I could hear Nathan's breaths quicken as he scanned the darkness. 'Where is he? God damn it...' he whispered under his breath.

"I strained my eyes, staring into the darkness for any sign of someone or something. There was a black blanket rolled up in a corner of the room and out of the corner of my eye, the shadow of a tree passed by the window. 'I don't see anything... Maybe it was a loose frame?' I couldn't imagine any other explanation.

"His hands did not slacken from the gun. It glistened in the moonlight, searching for its target. 'I'm going to start checking the rooms alright, could you clean up the broken glass? After I take a good look around, I'll go downstairs and get a board for that window,' he said through clenched teeth. He opened the drawer by our couch and found a flashlight to help him as he started exploring the first floor.

"I hurried into the kitchen and took out a small broom and bin to sweep the glass into. The wind began once more, but it was of no comfort with a broken window. Its chilled and hurt my ribs as I bent over to sweep. The breeze sounded like the rasping breaths of a man, with a whistle then a gust of wind in a constant rhythm. As I worked, there was a constant flicker in the corner of my eye, but every time I turned my head, there was nothing. I began to have the terrible feeling that someone was watching me. The looming fear from the eyes of the unknown was too great for me to try and call out to Nathan.

"The breeze grew steadily louder. I looked outside to see the trees dance in the distance, but instead I was greeted by a pair of round black eyes staring straight at me through the broken window. My blood froze, and my heart skipped a beat. It stared and breathed, pressing upon where the window once was. He had no face, but he had eyes. The moonlight fell upon him but would not illuminate his features. His shoulders did not end but were a part of the darkness. It was the silhouette and eyes of a man, but all the other features were indistinguishable from the night's oppressive blackness. He stood silent, staring at me.

"I began to scream frantically as I saw the shadow of a hand stretch through the broken window and work its way across the floor toward me. Springing to my feet, I began to sprint to the stairs. By the third step, I felt an ice-cold hand grip my ankle tightly. It felt like its grasp could crush my bones. I tried to resist it but it pulled my leg back with a flick of its wrist. My chin crashed into the stairs and my whole world went black as my eyes rolled back into my skull.

"I opened my eyes and saw myself outstretched on the stairs, unconscious. There was no longer anyone in the room with me. I turned and sat upright on the step, desperately trying to calm down. The television was on with nothing but static on the screen. Its sound felt like sandpaper rubbing against my skull. Through its craze inducing static, I began to hear a rustle beside me and voices all around me. I looked to my left and saw the small blanket was carelessly discarded on the floor. I heard the scurrying of small feet in the next room where Nathan had begun his search.

"I pushed open the door to the next room and heard the tiny feet scampering off to my left. There was a flashlight on the nightstand. I grabbed the flashlight and flicked it on, pointing it to my left. The light cast a shadow of a child without ever illuminating the figure of a child. A high-pitched giggle filled the room. The light flickered and the shadow disappeared. I felt a tug on my arm. The hairs on the back of my neck stood on end. 'Run.... Run!' It began to repeat this louder and louder until it was screaming at me. The whole world around me began to shake and dissipate into darkness as the screaming grew louder.

"My eyes could no longer see anything. 'Lily, Oh my God... Lily are you alright? Please baby, answer me!' pleaded Nathan from a distance. I felt cold, and tasted iron in my mouth. Then there was a hand on my shoulder. It was so warm and comforting. Next, I felt a warm breath on my face. Nathan's voice was no longer so far away.

"I opened my eyes and saw his milky hazel eyes staring at me with dilated pupils. 'Thank God you're alright Lily. We need to get out of here. I think we should just go to your brother's house. He's only a 35-minute drive away.' After my nightmare, I just wanted to leave my house. I wrapped my arms around him and held tight as he helped me stand. 'I just have to get the keys to the car alright? They're upstairs, you stay here, and I'll come right back. Here's my gun just in case he comes back,' he whispered in my ear. His eyes danced side to side, searching for the culprit of the night.

"I watched him with a heavy heart as he ascended the stairs. I wanted to go with him, but my legs would not listen. I wanted to tell him that I loved him, but my lips would not move. I was consumed with fear. All I could do was quickly shift my eyes to the window where the strange apparition of a man had been. The cold handle of Nathan's Glock was of little comfort against such an unrelenting knight in the dark.

"I heard his footsteps coming back from our room, approaching the stairs. Then his footsteps stopped. I kept listening tensely, staring at the window in apprehension all the while. It felt like on the second glance I could see it. I thought I could see its eyes, still staring back at me. I rubbed my eyes and looked at the window; there was nothing there.

"Minutes passed, but Nathan's footsteps did not resume. I ascended the stairs gingerly to investigate. I could see light shining out from under a closed door in the hallway. I quickly looked both ways down our hallway before approaching the door. I slowly turned the knob and opened the door; it gave an unpleasant screech like a bat as it turned and began to give way."

I began to sob. James passed me another glass of water with Kleenex. "I know it's hard. I've been there too," there was a dark, distant look in his eyes as he handed me the glass of water with a Kleenex. I dabbed my eyes with Kleenex and started drinking the water thirstily.

I could still feel its eyes on me while I sat in this diner with James. I would always feel his eyes unless I help James stop him so continued my story.

"Nathan laid on the floor, blue in the face with a red neck. The keys were right under my feet and the flashlight was still in his hands. The closet door was ajar in the room. I took the keys off the floor, withholding a scream. I knew he was in the room with me; I could feel it. It felt impossible, like a nightmare that just couldn't be real, but then I looked down at Nathan and his glossy fish eyes.

"The closet door began to slowly creak open. I could see his black eyes again, gleaming without light. Staring without truly comprehending, more akin to an animal's stare than a human's. I raised the gun and fired off ten rounds into the closet. The bullets just passed through the dark shadows and into the wall behind him. His silhouette began to tremble as it drifted toward me. I instinctually fired off another five rounds in rage, again to no avail.

"The gun's chamber clicked back; it was empty. I turned in a panic and slammed my shoulder into the door's frame, dropping the empty Glock onto the hard floor with a clank. Ahead of me, I saw the massive shadow of the figure, cast by the flashlight. The light flickered off, but the shadow ahead of me remained. From the walls, I saw its hands come out and take form. His hands looked like they were encircled by thousands of tiny black flies, never completely solid in form. I turned toward the stairs and grabbed hold of the railing with my right hand and held tightly to the keys with my other.

"His icy hands grabbed onto my right wrist. His grip was straining my wrist as he tried to pull me back upstairs. His arms were far stronger than mine; I began to remember Nathan's dead body lying on the floor. A shock went down my spine as the thought of this intruder wringing my neck crossed my mind. It was either him or me. I placed two keys between my fingers and swung at his face with all of my might.

"The keys were about to pop his black eyes when his grip completely released without warning. I swiped violently with my keys, but they passed through his face as I fell backwards down the stairs. His vaporous hands were still clenched. I rolled to the bottom of the stairs, everything hurt, but I forced myself to get up and out of the broken window.

"I was galloping across our front yard in the dead of night. My slippers felt soggy from the morning dew. They dug into the floor and tripped me. I broke my fall with my hands and looked back in panic. My head reared from the sudden snap back. In the house I saw it staring at me through the upstairs window where Nathan had been killed. Its face was still indiscernible, his whole being was only a shadow of a man. At the downstairs' window, I saw the face of a small child staring at me. I could not make out eyes, but this figure was shorter and seemed to have lips that bore a sadistic smile.

"I scrambled onto my feet and ran to my car in the drive-way. Once the doors were locked and the car was on, I took one last look at the house. They were both still there, watching me. Making sure I would leave them. The child was leering at me. I hated the smile it bore. I backed out of the driveway, hitting our mailbox just before I sped down the road.

"And after all that, now I'm here, sitting with you in this shabby diner," I sighed with some relief as I looked about me at the homely West Virginian diner James had chosen to meet in. He was finishing the last bite of his apple pie as I finished my story. James put down his memo pad to look at me. My cheeks became soaked by a salty river of tears. James couldn't bring back my husband no matter how kind or empathetic he turned out to be.

"I think the last part of your story was the most interesting for me. The man had a tight grip on your wrist until you tried to hit him where he not only let go but did not take the hit. It seems this thing could choose whether he was solid or not. But I think what is more reasonable, considering how he withheld his form, is that he perhaps was choosing which dimension he would reside in," suggested James with a raised eyebrow. "Secondly, I know those two men you described by their MO's. The little one is no child, it's just a midget with a sick sense of humor. We used to go... way back so to speak." He gave a heavy sigh with a gone look in his eyes. As if he was remembering someone or something from a distant past. "About your husband, I'm truly sorry. It's... It's really hard to lose someone you care so much about. Nothing will ever bring them back, but at least we will always have our memories of them, and a feeling in our hearts that reminds us that they're never gone." His eyes shimmered from welled up tears. He wouldn't let them fall, but instead he bore their pain, stinging his eyes without the relief of letting go. I could tell he had lost someone precious to him too.

"Thank you," I whispered back. I couldn't push back the choking feeling in my throat enough to speak louder. "I'm sorry for whoever you lost too." He gave a faint smile as he nodded his head.

"I'm going to stop this. They don't belong here," he replied with a snarl. Something had awoken in him, a will to fight. "I know exactly what I need to do, but I'll need your help." I nodded vigorously.

One of my husband's friends from the police force suggested a private investigator they worked with in extreme cases, but before I could call, I met James at the diner and he just took an interest in my case. It was a lucky coincidence.

We were back at the house by sundown. James calmly entered the house and I nervously followed. The door slammed shut behind us. The midget peeked out of the other room at us and the man stood at the top of the stairs, staring down at us. "If they move, shoot," James commanded. He pulled out his homemade EMP from under his coat and charged it. The man atop the stairs began to drift toward us, I could hear a growling sound. I looked behind me, expecting a dog. The door was still shut. Cold hands wrapped around my neck. "Back off!" A knife cut my shoulder from behind, but the hands released. The shadow retreated back to the staircase.

I heard an electric discharge beside me. When I turned, I saw an empty adjoining room and staircase.

"I'm sorry about that," I said, realizing my mistake in hesitating to shoot had endangered us both. James was clutching his head. His eyes were shut tightly from some apparent head trauma, although he looked untouched.

"It's alright, I'm sorry I had to cut you. The EMP was still charging, I had to do something to make it let you go. Ugh, that thing gets me every time." I felt fine despite James feeling awful.

"Why'd the EMP work?" I asked.

"Their dimension runs parallel to ours but somehow, they force their existence to run perpendicular so that they may intercept both dimensions. That's why they only appear to us as 'Shadow people,' their true forms are only visible at the source. This EMP disrupted that delicate existence and shifted them back into their parallel dimension. They could try to come back, but the odds of them intersecting our dimension here again is nearly impossible," he reassured me. "Their crime spree won't cross over today."

He left out the front door, into the night. I remembered that I drove us back to my house. I went to look outside to offer him a ride and thank him, but when I called out to James, all I saw was a dark figure looking down at some silver object in his hand that glittered in the moonlight before vanishing.

About Abdul H. Akbaryeh:

I was an avid reader since I was young. My first favorite book was Watership Down. I was raised in Maryland and I speak Farsi, English, and I am learning Spanish. By trade, I am an internal medicine physician.

I started writing in middle school when my mom said no more video games during the week. My first published novel came out at the end of high school, "A Hero's Plight."

I sought poetry as a therapy throughout college and medical school. I continued to write poetry and horror stories. My favorite writers are H.P. Lovecraft and Edgar Allan Poe for their beautiful styles of writing that make stories feel like poetry.

Feel free to visit my website for more upcoming work and updates at ahaAuthor.com

ABOUT THE ARTIST

Cover art was done by a Peruvian artist named Edy Rios. He is an extremely talented gentleman with a passion for water color paintings. He prides himself on painting while in nature to keep his mind clear and his art pure.

Cover design was a collaborative effort between my artist, wife, brother in law, and myself. Thank you to everyone's contributions!

THINGS TO COME

Now that I have finished medical residency, I plan on spending more time writing. A Walk into the Void is the start of a 9 book series that I have planned out for many years now. The characters and the world came together naturally. This will be the first of many adventures for James Amon. The next novel will be a different kind of horror story, "A Hunter's Solace." For those that may have read "A Hero's Plight," its continuation will also be in the works as it was a planned trilogy.

I hope you enjoyed my return to writing, I hope to continue to create stories filled with mystery and excitement. I hope in my characters, you too may find the hope and strength to persevere through whatever challenges you face.